Rat Run

Fear, when faced.
Often proves groundless.

Rat Run, is dedicated to the delightful pet rats, that over
the years I've had the privilege of owning and loving.

Rat Run

This is a work of fiction. Any resemblance to actual people and places is totally coincidental.

Cover image and design by Rebecca Fyfe
Interior illustrations by Y I Lee

The word rats spelled backwards is "star" and indeed they are in many ways. They make great pets for children and adults alike.

Glossary

The male rat is called a buck

A female rat is called a doe

Baby rats are known as kittens.

Generally, when a rat is happy, it will grind its teeth and bobble its eyes.

Their front paws are like small hands, and amazingly dexterous.
If it is cross, a rat will make a huffing sound.

When threatening another rat, fluffing the fur and twitching the tail, makes for an intimidating sight.

Most of the things the rats do in this story, they would do naturally.

Rat Run

Part One

Chapter One

After the warmth of the day, the cool of evening refreshed the inhabitants of Windom Woods. High in a tree, a Blackbird's song floated on the air.

Away in the distance, humans could be heard mowing their lawns.

As the sun slipped towards the horizon, the nocturnal inhabitants of the Woods prepared for another night of hunting.

Safe in their den, below the roots of an old oak tree; the rats slowly stirred. A buzz of excitement filtered through the den, as everyone focused on the arrival of the Princess. The same topic was on everyone's lips; what will she look like…when is she coming?

Finding the right female for the King's son, Piper, had taken time, but at last it was arranged.

Prince Piper, a handsome young buck, with a coat the colour of soft mink, snuggled close to his brother, Prince Malar. The two young brothers spent a lot of time together. Malar a big black buck was the more outgoing of the two, and much admired by the young females.

Stirring themselves, the two Princes' groomed each other and discussed the imminent arrival of the Princess, but their conversation was rudely interrupted, when a black female bounced into the chamber.

Sighing, Piper whispered in Malar's ear. "Troubles arrived."

Glancing at his sister, Malar grunted. "Go away, we are busy."

Tilting her head, Pecan's dark eyes studied them. "No you're not."

The Princes' rolled their eyes and carried on grooming, hoping if they ignored her, she might disappear.

The boisterous young Princess was no pushover, as her brothers often found to their cost. Whenever they argued, which was frequent Pecan would always have the last word.

"She will change," her father would say. "When she grows up, and a good buck comes into her life."

Pecan's response was always the same. "Ugh, you must be joking. I'm happy as I am thank you!" Glistening with indignation, she would throw her head up, huff loudly, and stomp away.

Piper sighed as Pecan plonked herself beside him. Studying him she asked. "Are you nervous about meeting the Princess?"

Piper shrugged. "Not really. Father's told me a little about her." Lowering his head, he stared at the ground.

Malar and Pecan waited, eager to hear what their father had told him.

Embarrassed, Piper continued to stare at his paws.

Irritated by his brother's silence, Malar nudged him "Go on tell us," he insisted. "What's she like?"

As Piper opened his mouth to speak, their aunt Freckle ambled into the chamber. Piper smiled with relief.

Giving him a nod, Freckle eased her old body into a comfortable position. Getting on in years, her dappled coat had lost its shine, it looked thin and patchy; but the attractive tear shaped spot on her forehead, still gave her a look of distinction. "Good morning, my little ones." She studied them through half closed eyes. "Have I interrupted something?"

Pecan's head bobbed with excitement. Glancing at her brothers, she said. "Piper was going to tell us about his Princess."

"Really," Freckle said with a knowing smile.

Piper glared at Pecan. "I only know what father has told me, and it's not much."

"Well, let me see if I can fill in some details," Freckle said chuckling at their expectant faces.

Piper's voice faltered, as he moved closer and asked. "Please aunt, tell me what she looks like."

Freckle gave him a reassuring smile. "Her coat is the colour of autumn leaves. She has a white triangle on her chest, and eyes as dark as the night sky."

Closing his eyes, Piper sighed. He was in love.

Malar grinned and poked him with a fisted paw.

Pecan squeaked with excitement. "Tell us more please," she pleaded. "We can't wait to meet her."

Aunty Freckle was about to tell her to sit still, when a huge presence filled the doorway. It was their father King Pierro. Crouching in obeisance, they watched him enter.

"What's all this then?" the King asked, trying to hide the twinkle in his ruby eyes.

Pecan rushed over and nuzzled against him. "Oh father; aunty Freckle has been telling us about Piper's princess."

"Has she now." Raising a brow he glanced at Freckle.

Lowering her head, Freckle peered at him through her lashes. Seeing the warmth in his eyes, she relaxed.

"What's her name father?" Pecan asked.

"Her name is Shamrock."

Piper's tail twitched with excitement. "When is she coming father?"

"Your question is the reason I am here. I've received word from her father, King Ludus. It appears the Princess and her party will be leaving first thing in the morning. Their journey will be dangerous. We can only hope the wild rats of Tamwood are unaware of our plans. I will be sending a party of Bucks, to meet them halfway for safety. Loki will lead, as he knows the area well."

"Can I go too father, please?" Piper asked.

"Me too," Malar exclaimed...always eager for an adventure.

"I will consider it," the King said. Turning, he left the chamber; his champagne coat glistened in a shaft of light filtering through a gap in the tree roots above.

❦❦❦

Later that evening, Loki, a large battle scarred buck, huddled in a dark area of the den. Crouched round him were the four rats he had chosen to join him in the morning. Not many perhaps, but those four might as well be six; so great was their courage.

Rupert and Domino were the youngest. They were brothers and extremely close, both variegated, like aunty Freckle...not surprising, as she was a distant relative.

Bluebear, a huge black buck sat beside them. His dark eyes fixed on Loki. Bluebear and Loki trusted each other implicitly. In their younger days, they had played a large part in protecting the den and the King.

Domino and Rupert were learning a lot from these two old soldiers. They knew tomorrow would be no exception.

"We will be making an early start," Loki declared, having a quick scratch behind his left ear. "We must stick close together," he warned.

"Are you anticipating problems?" Bluebear asked.

"Possibly," Loki said, "I am concerned about the wild rats of Tamwood. They are always on the lookout for ways to steal our females. If they succeed tomorrow, that would be a real coup for them, so we must stay alert at all cost."

"I'm looking forward to it," Rupert squeaked. "I would relish the chance to reap revenge on a wild rat or two."

Domino, the cautious one of the two, paused in his tail washing and muttered under his breath. "One of these days you won't be so keen."

Loki tutted before continuing; his deep frown making it clear...he was concerned. "Be aware, this task could be perilous. Be sure to watch each other's backs."

With nods of agreement they paired up to do some mutual grooming.

⮞⮞⮞

In the rest of the den the nightly activity was getting underway. Youngsters could be heard play fighting, with lots of squeaks and protests, as someone played too rough. Others were chatting. In hushed tones they complained about leaving their human owner. "Food was always available then," one of the rats grumbled. "Now we're forced to scavenge for it."

Curled up in a dark corner, Freckle tried to ignore their complaints. It was the same every night. The older rats chose to forget the horror of that night. Thinking about it, the hair on Freckle's spine stood on end. She would never forget the scratching and squeaking, as the wild rats invaded their shed.

Squeezing through a hole, the wild rats raided the food sack, before turning their attention to Freckle and the other rats cowering in their cages. In no time the wild rats bit through the thin wire securing the cage doors.

Freckle's body shook at she recalled the frightening events of that night. She could not erase the squeals of terror from her memory, as the wild rats attacked and killed so many young males and babies. Even now, after all this time, she had no idea how she escaped…no idea how she and a group of terrified young females, found themselves huddled beneath a pile of wood a few yards from the shed that had been their home, but which now was a place of death and mayhem.

Her heart raced, as she remembered seeing a young Pierro followed by a few other males, Bluebear among them, racing towards the wood pile. Their presence instilled calm. Freckle almost smiled as she remembered how Pierro automatically took control of the situation. The frightened rats were desperate for leadership, so no one challenged him.

It was Pierro who led them on a desperate race through the night, until they entered the woods and found their present home. For a long time they lived on a knife edge, wondering if the wild rats would find them…they never did. Pierro eventually became King…their numbers increased and life took on a semblance of normality.

Sitting on her haunches, Freckle raised a paw and brushed away a tear. Hatred coursed like fire through her veins. The vision of her two small daughters dragged away by the scruff of the neck, enraged her. Their cries of terror plagued her dreams.

Freckle hoped one day before she was too old, she might have the chance to take revenge on those who took her daughters and destroyed her life. Swishing her tail, she stood to her feet, shook the dust from her coat and joined the others foraging. In between mouthfuls, Freckle chastised them for their ingratitude and grumbling.

❦❦❦

In the lower depths of the den, King Pierro sat in his chamber with Piper and Malar. His brow furrowed as he tried to explain, why Malar could accompany the bucks, but not Piper.

"We are investing a lot in you Piper; I need to be sure you are safe. The best way to do that is to keep you here. I am sorry; I know you want to go, but it is far too dangerous."

"So why can Malar go?" Piper protested. "He's as valuable as me."

King Pierro agreed, but explained Malar would be in the care of Loki and Bluebear. "I cannot afford to lose two sons if the worst should happen." Turning to Malar the King warned him to do everything he was told by the other bucks. Malar's promise brought a relieved smile to the King's face.

Dismissed by their father, the two princes left the chamber walking side by side, Malar jubilant…Piper downcast.

"Don't worry," Malar encouraged "Your turn will come soon enough."

"I know, but I so want to go; its ages since I've had an adventure."

Malar tried to cheer him up as they joined the rest of the clan foraging for food. Sitting together in a dandelion patch, they chewed the tasty leaves, their minds occupied with thoughts of what tomorrow might bring.

༄༄༄

The next morning, Windom woods lay shrouded in mist. Like a ghostly grey spectre, the mist floated among the trees, its cold fingers chilling the huddled rats. The eerie silence and absence of bird song, made everyone nervous.

Under the watchful eye of King Pierro, Loki and his small group made their farewells and hurried away from the den. They quickly disappeared, swallowed by the swirling mist.

Keeping to the edge of the forest path, the small group kept low and moved fast. Old Bluebear puffed a little. He was basically fit, but age had put some weight on him. Keeping close to Loki's tail, he was followed by Prince Malar, Rupert and Domino.

"I'm grateful for this mist," Bluebear whispered. "It should work to our advantage."

"I hope you're right," Loki replied. "The problem could be when we reach the open meadow."

Rupert shouted from the back. "Is that where we are meeting them?"

"Yes, keep your voice down," Bluebear warned.

No more was said. Running as fast as they could, they used the tall grass and hedges as cover.

Rats are not normally active during the day, it's time for resting after a busy night foraging; but these were exceptional circumstances. King Pierro and his advisors had agreed, going in daylight might be safer. There would certainly be fewer predators and those who were up and about, would not expect rats to be running around in broad daylight.

Chapter Two

Deep in his den, on the edge of Athston woods, King Ludus was busy preparing for his daughter's journey.

Situated among bushes and trees the den was well hidden. Nevertheless, Athston could be a dangerous place. A couple of unfriendly weasels lived nearby. Also a dog fox occasionally roamed the area. Not to mention hungry owls always on the lookout for a tasty meal. A large plump rat was always a welcome treat. Great care was the order of the day. Hence, the King and his advisors felt the Princess's journey would be a little safer in daylight, when hopefully most predators would be sleeping.

King Ludus summoned Coco, a large fawn buck into his chamber; there was a lot to discuss. Coco waited patiently, while the King chose the three bucks that would accompany him and the princess.

"Ah Coco, good to see you, do come in. I believe you know Captain, Percy, and Oscar."

Coco acknowledged the three rats with a nod of his head.

Captain, a huge white buck, with black head and shoulders, towered over the two rats standing beside him. Lumbering towards Coco, he bowed his head. "It is an honour to serve with you," he said.

Percy, a large silver fawn and Oscar a smaller white rat, followed his lead.

All three were brave and had great respect for Coco. They had seen him deal severely with any outside rat threatening the safety of the den. Captain had fought alongside him on numerous occasions.

Taking their places in front of the King, they waited to receive their instructions.

King Ludus's eyes narrowed as he stared from one to the other. Fixing his gaze on Coco, he said. "You are in charge and will lead the party. Surround the princess and her companion Crystal at all times." His tail swished as he gazed round at them. "Is that understood?"

"Yes, Your Highness," they said, lowering their eyes.

"I am sure there will be no problems," Coco said confidently.

"Even so," the King replied. "Be cautious. Do not drop your guard for a second. There will be many dangers, not least the wild rats from Tamwood." The King frowned, his fur stood on end at the thought of them.

Rising on his hind legs, Coco declared. "Fear not your highness; we will protect the princess with our lives."

The others nodded in agreement.

Taking a calming breath, the King said softly. "I know. She could not be with braver bucks. Go now and rest. You will need to be refreshed and alert in the morning." Bowing low, Coco led the others from the chamber.

Watching them leave, King Ludus called to mind memories of the past…memories of his escape with Pierro on that dark night, the night the wild rats broke into their shed.

Ludus sighed. He liked Pierro; as youngsters they had shared a cage and got on extremely well. But after the wild rat attack, they were forced to grow up quickly. Their survival and that of the rats with them depended on it. Over time, they both realised only one of them could rule. Rather than come to blows, and risk serious injury, Ludus decided to leave and take his chances elsewhere.

So one dark night, he and three young females left Pierro's den and journeyed in search of a new home. They had no idea where they were going. Three days it took to find the appropriate place...three days filled with terror! Predators appeared out of the woodwork...foxes, stoats, sharp eyed hawks hovering in the sky above, and owls, gliding through the night on silent wings of death. The youngest female died in the talons of an owl.

Ludus trembled; he could still hear her final scream. However, the experience contributed to making him a strong leader, the rightful King. Massive in build... battle scarred from his many fights; he held his hard won position in the den with help from loyal bucks like Coco.

Ludus knew he needed this alliance with King Pierro. Through his daughter, Princess Shamrock, his family line would be strengthened. Over time, more bucks would be born, reinforcing his hold on this area of Athston and helping against the growing attacks from the wild rats in the forest of Tamwood.

King Pierro and his clan were known for their build and strength. King Ludus needed an injection of new blood into his family line. However, success depended on his daughter reaching King Pierro's den safely.

Ludus sat at the den's entrance, staring into the darkness. High in a tree an owl hooted. In the distance a fox barked. Ludus' ears twitched to every sound. Raising his head he sniffed the air, so much nocturnal activity. *Just as well they are leaving in daylight*, he thought. *It will still be dangerous, but perhaps a few less enemies to worry about.*

Feeling a little more relaxed, he groomed his thick brown coat and tried not to think about the coming journey that lay ahead for his daughter, Shamrock.

❦❦❦

The following morning, they were greeted by a cold swirling mist. Ludus's heart raced as he bade farewell to his daughter, and watched her disappear into the forest.

Shamrock's body tingled; her rapid breathing formed a misty cloud around her head. Her friend Crystal, a small white rat with bright dark eyes, fussed and fidgeted as the bucks formed a circle around them. With Coco in the lead, they made a dash for the cover of the trees. Once there, they were able to regroup.

Keeping low and close together, they ran from cover to cover, eyes and ears tuned to every sight and sound; their lives depended on it. The mist shrouding the woods helped a lot, but they knew, eventually the rising sun would burn it away. They needed to be in the meadow before that happened.

They were making good time. Little Crystal was tired but able to keep up. Shamrock, an energetic racy doe, coped well.

They were moving fast, when all of a sudden Coco stopped in his tracks, causing them to bump into him.

Shamrock and Crystal tried to smother their giggles.

"Shush!" Coco whispered. Attempting to hide his embarrassment, he sat and had a quick scratch.

Ahead was a small break in the trees; already the mist was beginning to clear.

"What's wrong?" Captain asked. "Why have we stopped?"

"I don't know. I just have a bad feeling," Coco said softly.

"Shall I go ahead and take a look?" Oscar asked. Being the youngest, he was keen to impress.

Coco nodded, but warned him to be careful.

Oscar made a dash for the bushes; crouching low he could hardly be seen.

After what seemed like ages to the waiting rats, a loud scream shattered the tense silence. Trembling, everyone shot to their feet.

Princess Shamrock and Crystal huddled together.

Coco's hair stood on end, his tail twitched like a snake. Herding the Princess and Crystal into some thick ferns for safety, he left Captain and Percy in charge. "Stay here, while I go and see what's happened." Moving cautiously, he followed the direction of the cry.

Coco's heart pounded as he reached the spot and saw Oscar's lifeless body caught in a metal trap; his white coat spattered with blood. He'd stumbled into a rabbit trap. The sharp teeth gripped him by the shoulder, piercing his lung.

Coco swallowed hard, he had no idea if there were more traps ahead of them, but they had to keep going, he looked around to be sure it was safe. Then standing on his hind legs, he summoned the others.

Cautiously, they moved towards him, trying to walk exactly where he had. Coco moved away from the trap so they wouldn't see it; especially the two does.

Everyone was trembling and breathing hard when they reached him. Taking a brief rest, they listened as Coco explained what had happened to Oscar.

Shamrock's voice faltered as she said. "Oh dear, that's awful."

"It is, Princess; but I believe it was quick." Raising his head, Coco stared at their anxious faces. "We need to move on," he urged. "Once we are back in the woods, the meadow is not far away."

They were relieved to hear this and keen to get going, so one buck down, they continued their journey.

It seemed to take forever to reach the shelter of the woods ahead of them. But once under the canopy of leaves, and hidden by tall bracken, they relaxed and their pace quickened.

The sun was high in the sky by the time they reached the edge of the meadow. It opened out before them lush and green. An array of wild flowers swayed gently in the soft breeze; their sweet perfume scented the air.

The little group stopped behind Coco. Lifting their heads they listened, their small pink ears twitching to every sound.

"It seems okay," Percy whispered.

"Yes, it does," Coco said. "Nevertheless, we will stay close to the hedge, and hopefully meet up with King Pierro's bucks soon." He felt confident, but knew it was wise to be cautious. Apart from the sad loss of Oscar, he was pleased how well the journey had gone. *Maybe there will be no trouble after all, and everything will go according to plan.* Encouraged by the thought, he led his little group into the meadow.

The birds were singing, and the warm sun on their backs felt good.

Gazing round, Coco breathed a sigh of relief, yet he couldn't quell a strange unease…couldn't dismiss the uncomfortable tightening in his stomach. "Stay low," he whispered to the others. Crouched in the long grass they waited, alert…senses tuned for danger.

Chapter Three

Deep in Tamwood forest, the wild rats lived in a maze of tunnels and chambers, dug underneath a large ancient oak. The den was concealed by tall trees, impenetrable brush, and bracken.

Inside the main chamber, King Flylord, a massive, heavily scarred black rat, with small piercing eyes, paced to and fro, dragging his thick tail behind him.

Crouched in front of him, two mangy weasels called Werzal and Wart, trembled as they watched him pace.

King Flylord had coerced them into spying for him. They informed him if anything unusual occurred at the dens in Athston and Windom woods. However, this time they'd slipped up. They delayed bringing the news about the goings on between King Ludus, and Pierro.

Flylord huffed; he could hardly contain his fury. *How am I supposed to do anything, with such short notice?*

The two weasels flinched, and huddled together as he swung round on them, his yellow teeth bared...eyes blazing.

"You should have told me sooner," he hissed. With his fur fluffed up, he looked twice as large.

With squeaky voices they apologised, and flattened themselves closer to the ground. They were aware of the other rats standing around them, their eyes glued to King Flylord. One word from him and the weasels knew they were dead.

Calming himself, Flylord demanded to know everything.

Once the weasels had shared their information, they were roughly escorted from the premises…grateful to have escaped in one piece. Making a dash into the undergrowth, they recuperated, before going rabbit hunting.

Inside the rats den, the air was thick with tension. King Flylord's voice quivered with suppressed anger, as he put his plan of action to the bucks surrounding him.

"We don't have much time, so we'll have to move fast. It seems Loki, and Bluebear, are leading a party to meet this princess. We've tangled with them before, so I warn you to watch your step. If what the weasels say is true, one of the King's sons will also be with them. I don't want anyone to escape, deal with them all. Then bring the princess here to me; Zadock and Jet will be in charge." He glared at them. "Don't let me down," he hissed.

With a quick nod, the two bucks turned aggressively to the others.

Zadock spoke first. "Follow us, do everything we say, and there will be no problems. If you don't pull your weight, you will have me to answer to." The threat in his voice was unmistakable. Fluffing his fur, he narrowed his piggy eye at them. Zadock's bad temper was well known, and having suffered the loss of an eye in one of his many fights, his unpleasant appearance added credence to his words.

"And me," Jet snapped. Flattening his ears, he shoved Zadock with his shoulder. Huffing and twitching their tails, the pair faced each other.

Frustrated with their constant bickering and jockeying for position, Flylord snapped. "Don't start fighting among yourselves. Get out and remember what I said. I will see you before you leave at dawn."

As they filed out, the King's young son, Prince Timere came in to see him, followed by his sister Princess Liza.

"Where is Seamist?" Flylord asked. She was their half-sister, and the King's favourite; although he tried to hide the fact.

Liza's lip twisted in a snarl. "The last time I saw her, she was playing with our cousins."

The King stared at his two offspring. Neither of them were what you would call well-built, in fact Prince Timere, compared to his sister Liza, was undeniably small. Timere's fragile build was a worry to his father, hence the need for an injection of fresh blood into the family. *I really need this princess for my son, we must not fail.*

"Where are the bucks going father?" Timere asked.

"It's a secret at the moment my son, but you will know soon enough."

"Can I go with them father, can I?" Liza asked. Fluffing her fur, she beat up Timere, who squeaked a loud protest.

"Stop that at once!" Flylord shouted. "You are a doe, behave like one."

"I'm as strong as him," she said sneering at her brother.

That wouldn't be hard, the King thought. His face softened with sympathy as he stared at Timere. "Don't you worry son, soon we will have a nice strong female for you." A brief smile flashed in Flylord's eyes. He was fond of his young son, and wanted the best for him, even if it meant having to kidnap a female from another clan.

"So, can I go father?" Liza persisted. "I won't get in the way, really I won't,"

Gazing at her, the King's eyes filled with pride. "You can go, but hear me, stay at the back and keep out of harm's way."

"I will father, I promise." Squeaking with excitement, Liza bounced around the chamber. She had no idea what sort of mission the bucks were going on, or how dangerous it might be. She just loved adventures. And secretly she enjoyed being around Zadock; which she knew would infuriate her father, had he known.

King Flylord's eyes narrowed as a thought flashed into his mind. *It could be good to have a female there. The captured princess won't feel so afraid.* Raising a paw, he stroked his long whiskers. *Seamist would be a better choice. She is gentler than Liza. But this situation needs someone who can handle themselves, and Liza can certainly do that.*

Slumped on his ample haunches, Flylord nibbled on some seed. His ears twitched to every sound in the den, and surrounding forest.

Liza and Timere had departed, Liza to get herself ready and Timere to have a lie down.

Flylord's dark eyes glinted, as he anticipated the arrival of the princess for his son. *It is a shame it has to be this way, but this princess is just what we need.*

Outside his den, soft morning light slowly emerged above the horizon. The forest resounded to the dawn chorus greeting the new day.

Rising to his feet, Flylord shook the dust from his coat, and went to meet the bucks and Liza.

Liza rubbed affectionately against him. "Thank you for letting me go, father," she purred.

"Make sure you stay close to the bucks, do you understand me?"

"Yes, I promise. Don't worry father."

"Humph," Flylord grunted. Staring at her through narrowed eyes, he found it hard to believe she would obey him.

Facing the excited bucks, Flylord sat on his haunches and called them to order. "If you leave now, you should reach the meadow before Loki and the other party arrive. Kill them all, but do not harm the Princess." Raising his paws, he dismissed them. "Go!" He shouted.

❈❈❈

Back in the meadow, Loki and his party had arrived, they were eager to meet the princess, and escort her to King Pierro. Feeling relaxed, they took a few minutes to have a wash and brush-up; unaware of the danger ahead of them.

Hiding under a shrub, at the edge of the woods, eight brown bodies crouched low, well hidden by the long grass. Eight pairs of eyes watched, as Coco and his party moved into the meadow, and made their way towards Loki.

Chapter Four

Crouched under the shrub, Zadock's tail swished with excitement. "Let them meet up, then we will make our move," he hissed.

"What about Princess Liza?" Jet asked. Scowling, he glared at her.

"What about her?" Zadock snapped. "She can take care of herself, and anyway, I've told her what to do, so leave her be, we'll need her later."

Hearing their conversation, Liza narrowed her eyes at Jet and huffed with annoyance. Nevertheless, she had to admit, if she'd realized what sort of mission the bucks were going on, she wouldn't have been so keen to join them.

The wild rats knew it would take a while for the two parties to meet, so they decided to follow, keeping low and quiet. Being brown in colour they blended in well with their surroundings. The two parties ahead had no idea the danger they were in.

❧❧❧

It seemed to take forever for the two groups to meet. Keeping close to the hedge for protection, there were lots of excited squeaks as they greeted each other.

Prince Malar struggled to quell his excitement as Coco introduced him to the Princess.

Peering at him under long lashes, Shamrock said softly. "Hello. Thank you for coming to meet me."

"It's a pleasure." Malar said with a warm smile. "We are so pleased you are coming to us. How was your journey?" Seeing the fleeting sadness in her eyes, he stepped closer. "Is something wrong?"

Raising her head, Shamrock's voice broke. "One of our bucks was killed in a trap. It was awful!"

Before Malar could comfort her, Coco and Loki called them to order.

Domino, Rupert, and Bluebear were keeping watch, with the two bucks from Coco's party.

"Right," Loki said. "We must be on our way, surround the does and let's get going."

As they were organising themselves and preparing to say goodbye to Coco and his party; the wild rats struck.

Emerging from the shadows, they fell on the startled rats. In an instant, the peaceful meadow erupted to the sound of battle…loud hissing and squeaking shattered the silence.

Huddled under the hedge, Princess Shamrock and Crystal flinched at the sight of flying fur and writhing bodies.

Domino fell first; a fatal wound to his neck. Seeing his brother fall, Rupert's blood boiled. Enraged, he killed one of the wild rats and turned just in time to see another coming at him from behind.

Loki was trapped by Jet, and another large buck close to the frightened does, which were backing even further into the hedge.

With the sharp nails on his back feet, Loki dispatched the one buck and quickly turned his attention to Jet, who was making a grab for his side. They locked in a deadly embrace, rolling around like a huge puffed up ball, fur flying everywhere.

Captain lumbered over and grabbed Jet by the back of the neck, shaking him like a rag doll.

But Jet hung on to Loki, until his last breath.

Hissing with rage, Captain continued to shake Jet, before dropping him on the ground.

Loki was badly hurt and lay beside the dead rat unable to move. "Help the others, Captain," he urged his voice breathless and weak.

Captain turned and fought alongside Coco and Bluebear.

Prince Malar lay injured in the grass, a deep wound in his shoulder.

Meanwhile Zadock was locked in a fierce battle with Rupert and Coco's buck, Percy. Dispatching Percy with a fatal blow to the neck, he turned his attention to Rupert who was beginning to tire, but fought bravely on.

Rupert was succumbing to Zadock's fearsome strength, when Coco appeared at his side. With teeth bared, Coco went for Zadock but missed.

Zadock swung round and lashed out with his back foot, his long nails ripping into Coco's side.

Rupert stood stunned as Coco lay dying. Crouching beside him, he fluffed his fur and twitched his tail, in an attempt to intimidate Zadock. It appeared to work as Zadock turned from him and went for Bluebear, who was standing in front of Shamrock and Crystal, attempting to protect them from two large rats, which were closing in fast.

Liza left the protection of the hedge and flew at Bluebear.

Her attack took him by surprise, but he managed to shake her off. The two large bucks grabbed him and Zadock joined in.

Old Bluebear fought for his life, but he knew the odds were against him.

Rupert, having got his second wind flew into the fray, taking one buck by surprise; he killed it with a bite to the neck, and then locked on to the other.

Zadock meanwhile, had inflicted a serious wound on Bluebear who lay on his side breathing hard.

Rupert fought bravely, as he tried to keep Zadock and the other buck away from the does. But a swift kick from Zadock sent him flying into the grass. Winded and bleeding, he lay where he fell. The sound of fighting grew faint, as darkness enveloped him, and he passed out.

Shamrock and Crystal made a dash for safety through the hedge, but Liza and a couple of the wild bucks headed them off, forcing them back to Zadock.

The wild rats had lost Jet, and three other bucks. Zadock was wounded but not seriously. He was still in charge. With Shamrock and Crystal, surrounded by Liza and the remaining bucks, he prepared to move off.

However, he noticed Prince Malar lying in the grass. "Get him," he shouted. "We will take him with us; he could be useful."

Unable to resist, Malar was forced to limp to the waiting group.

With Zadock in the lead, they disappeared into the woods, leaving behind the bodies of dead and injured rats.

Chapter Five

After the noise of battle, the silence was eerie. Rupert came round to feel something cold touching his ear. Holding his breath, he opened one eye, and saw two big brown eyes staring at him. A large rabbit was standing over him.

"Are you badly hurt?" The rabbit asked.

"I don't know," Rupert said. The rabbit's voice sounded distant.

"You need help; I will fetch my family." He hopped off and a few minutes later returned with three other rabbits.

Rupert managed to sit up, his ribs hurt and he'd lost some blood, but his wounds were not serious.

With the help of the rabbits he went around checking on the fallen rats.

"There's one alive, here," a rabbit shouted.

Rupert went to see; it was Bluebear. He was in a bad way.

Relieved to see Rupert, Bluebear tried to raise himself.

"You're hurt, don't move," Rupert said. Close by he noticed two other rats, they were injured but alive. It was Captain and Loki.

"Oh dear," he groaned. "What can I do? I need to get back to my den and tell my King what has happened, but how can I leave you all?"

Seeing his concern, the rabbits gathered round. "Don't worry, we will take them to our burrow, they will be safe there."

Rupert bowed his head in gratitude. "Thank you, I appreciate your help." Staring at them, he asked. "What are your names?"

The rabbit who had sniffed him answered. "My name is Sky, this is my sister Cloud, and these two are Muddle and Peewee."

"I'm pleased to meet you." Rupert trembled as a sudden chill brought on a feeling of weakness. Groaning he slumped in the grass. Every muscle ached, and breathing was painful.

"Look, you can't travel in your state," Cloud insisted. "You need rest and food. Come with us, all of you."

Slowly and painfully, the little party made their way further into the meadow, keeping in the long grass. Cloud took the lead; while Sky and the two large buck rabbits Muddle and Peewee, helped the weak and injured rats make the short journey to the burrow's entrance. Inside the burrow, it was dark and cool. Cloud led them to a small chamber, where comfy beds of soft moss and grass welcomed them.

Bluebear and Loki lay down together, grateful to be safe. Cloud fussed over them, making sure they had enough food and water. They were both badly hurt and too weak to eat, but more than grateful for the water.

Wincing with pain, Captain limped to join Rupert. His right back leg was broken.

Raising a paw, Rupert gently touched his shoulder. "Are you going to be alright?"

"I hope so," he said. His injured leg protruded at a strange angle as he sat and nibbled on a dandelion leaf.

Rupert furtively watched him...well aware a broken limb was bad news. Sitting close to Captain, he did his best to comfort him and made sure the food was within reach. They ate in silence; both traumatised from the battle, the loss of life and the capture of the Princess. Once they finished eating, Rupert did his best to help Captain settle down to rest.

Hearing Bluebear sigh, he went over to him. "How are you feeling?"

"I've felt better." He glanced across at Loki. "He's not good," he whispered.

"I know, neither is Captain."

Bluebear groaned. "This is a bad day, a bad day indeed!"

Nodding in agreement, Rupert lowered his head closer to Bluebear and whispered. "It will be dark soon. I will return to our den and tell King Pierro what has happened." His heart raced at the thought. His legs trembled, threatening to give way beneath him. Sucking in a breath, he peered at Bluebear. "You will be safe here, rest and heal."

Opening his eyes, Bluebear reached out a paw and touched Rupert's shoulder. "I'm sorry you have to go alone and take such dreadful news to the King."

Sky's large form filled the chamber. "He won't be alone," he said peering over Rupert's shoulder. "I will be with him. In fact I know a short cut; our burrow has a long passage that comes out in a place called Squirrel Wood, which is not so far from your den."

Tears of relief glistened in Rupert's eyes. "That's wonderful news! If possible I would like to leave as soon as the sun goes down." Staring blankly at the den wall, he frowned.

"What is it?" Bluebear asked.

"How am I going to explain the loss of Prince Malar and the Princess Shamrock to our King? We let the wild rats take them, we failed!"

Groaning, Bluebear raised his head. "Look, try not to worry, just get there safely."

Sky nodded in agreement. "Take one step at a time," he encouraged.

Overcome with exhaustion and shock, Rupert lay beside Bluebear, and for an hour or two he slept. When he woke he felt a little stronger, and his wound was no longer bleeding. Glancing at the others, he was pleased to see they were still sleeping; and old Bluebear was breathing more easily.

Quietly, Rupert left the chamber and found Sky outside the burrow, chatting with his sister, Cloud.

"Ah, there you are," Sky said. "I'm ready to go, if you are?" Smiling, he peered at Rupert. "I must say you look a little better. How are the others?"

"They are still sleeping," Rupert replied.

"Good, we'd best go then." Sky turned to Cloud. "Take good care of our guests, while are gone."

"I will, don't worry."

Sky turned to Rupert. "Come on, follow me," he said disappearing into the burrow.

Turning to Cloud, Rupert thanked her.

"I'm glad we are able to help." Nodding towards the burrows entrance, she said. "I suggest you follow him, he can get impatient." Smiling warmly, she bade him farewell.

Inside the burrow, Sky waited for him at the entrance to a dark tunnel.

Rupert squinted; he could hardly see a thing. However, as they ran down the long tunnel his eyes adjusted to the dim light. Running behind Sky, he focused on the rabbit's bobbing white tail. Neither of them said a word.

Twice, Sky stopped to listen, which gave Rupert a chance to catch his breath, as he was still weak from the battle. It seemed ages before Rupert saw a glimmer of moonlight up ahead. Drawing in a deep breath, he increased his pace.

Sensing Rupert's relief, Sky said. "We're nearly there." Reaching the exit, the rabbit stopped. "This comes out in squirrel territory, but they won't bother us if we keep moving. They will see we're not after their food and leave us alone. Are you ready?"

Rupert nodded.

They made a dash to the nearest bush. The moon was bright in a cloudless sky. A million stars twinkled in the vast blackness.

High in a tree, an owl hooted, sending a shudder through Rupert.

Seeing his anxiety, Sky said. "Stay close to me. If we go from cover to cover, we'll be safe."

"Lead on," Rupert said, grateful that Sky was with him.

They made their way through the dense wood, straining to hear every sound, their nerves taught. Half way through, they stopped to rest under a tree.

"Ouch!" Rupert exclaimed. Something hard hit him on the head. It turned out to be a nut, and was quickly followed by another.

Two large grey squirrels scooted down the trunk of the tree and appeared in front of them. "What are you doing in our woods?" they demanded.

Sky did his best to reassure them. "We are on our way to Windom woods. We need to get there as soon as possible," he said.

Peering at them, the squirrels muttered to each other, but seemed to accept the explanation and let them pass.

Sky and Rupert thanked them and continued their journey. In the distance they could see Windom woods.

Panting with exertion, Rupert forced himself to keep going. Every muscle screamed with pain, a wound on his shoulder re-opened and trickled blood. Exhausted, he was not sure he would make it.

Seeing the open wound, Sky gritted his teeth; glancing round, his long ears twitched at every sound, every rustle in the undergrowth. He knew the smell of blood would alert predators. "We need to stop and rest," he said.

Sighing with relief, Rupert collapsed under a bush.

"I won't be a minute," Sky said disappearing under a holly bush. Before Rupert had time to miss him, he re-appeared with a mouthful of leaves. "Here, put these on your wound."

Taking the leaves, Rupert studied them.

"They will stop the bleeding," Sky explained. "I'm concerned that predators will smell the blood and track us."

Rupert nodded; his paws trembled as he pushed the leaves over the seeping wound.

"Try not to move too much. Here, take these." He handed Rupert some nuts. Sky sat protectively close, nibbling tender grass shoots. They hadn't realized how hungry they were.

After eating, Rupert felt strengthened. Removing the leaves, he was relieved to see the wound had stopped bleeding. Carefully, he had a quick wash, he felt sure he must look a mess, his coat splattered with dry blood, and covered with deep scratches.

Sky watched him, fascinated by his white head spot and the black dapples over his back. "What exactly are you?" he asked. "I've only seen wild rats."

"I'm a variegated."

Sky's large brown eyes widened, as he exclaimed. "You're a what?"

Rupert smiled. "I'm a variegated. In my clan there are many different colours."

Sky's brow furrowed. "Do you all get on?"

"Yes, of course," Rupert replied.

"So why don't you get on with the wild rats?" Sky asked. "I mean, you are all rats, aren't you?"

"Good question. I really don't know." Rupert frowned. "As long as I can remember, it's always been like this. It's all we know. I wish it could be different."

Sky would have asked more questions, but an owl flew low over their bush; forcing them to scurry under cover.

They decided they'd better move on. So leaving the relative safety of the woods, they began the hazardous journey out in the open.

Rupert tried to remember the places of safety from the day before, when they had gone out to meet the Princess, but it all looked so different going the other way, and the scent trail they'd left was all but gone.

He exhaled with relief as they reached the edge of Windom woods and hurried in among the trees. His eyes brightened, as ahead he saw the den.

The joy of reaching home safely, lightened his step...eased the pain and tension in his muscles.

However, as he led Sky towards the den, his pace slowed as a cloud of doubt and sorrow engulfed him. No matter the joyous welcome they would receive. Rupert knew nothing would change the fact. He was the bearer of tragic news.

Chapter Six

It was late afternoon, when Zadock and his captives arrived at the den in Tamwood forest. The captives were terrified and exhausted. Particularly Prince Malar, pain and loss of blood had weakened him.

Liza had done her best to put Shamrock and Crystal at ease, but she had little success; neither doe trusted her.

In fact, Crystal took an instant dislike to her. Were it not for Zadock and the other bucks keeping watch over them, the two might well have come to blows.

The instant they entered the den, Malar was put under guard. His condition was not good. The journey had taken its toll. His captors made him as comfortable as possible. It was to their advantage, as they might need him as a bargaining chip.

Princess Shamrock and Crystal were placed in a comfortable chamber, where they were left to rest.

Liza's half-sister Seamist, took it upon herself to care for them, bringing them food and water.

Shamrock took to her instantly. She liked her quiet gentle nature, so unlike her sister Liza, who was, as Crystal put it, overly confident and in your face. A description, Shamrock found most amusing. Resting next to Crystal on a bed of dry grass, Shamrock watched Seamist place a bowl of water in the corner.

Seamist sensed Shamrock watching her. "Is there anything more I can do for you?" she asked.

"There is one thing," Shamrock said. "Could you check on Prince Malar for me? He's injured, and it would put my mind at rest."

Seamist nodded. "Of course, I will go now." She hurried to where Prince Malar was being held. The chamber was deeper in the den. "I wish to see the Prince," she said to the bucks guarding him.

Bowing their heads, they stepped aside.

Prince Malar lay in the corner, his eyes closed as though asleep. He looked up as she entered, even in his frail state, he liked what he saw…liked her golden brown fur, the white sock on her left foot and her lovely dark eyes. Remembering her sister Liza, he frowned. *Sisters and yet so different*, he thought to himself.

"How are you feeling, can I get you anything?" Seamist asked.

"Some more water please, and can you tell me if Princess Shamrock is alright?"

Seamist smiled, and assured him the princess was fine. "They both are," she said. "In fact, it was the princess who asked me to come and see you. She is concerned about you. I will go now and fetch you something to eat and drink." She left the chamber, but in a short while returned with food and water.

Prince Malar tried to eat a few of the nuts she brought him, but it was the water he really needed.

Seamist watched him drink. Even though one ear was torn, and there was a deep wound in his shoulder, he was a handsome buck. So different from most of the bucks in her den; who were aggressive, scruffy, and predominantly the same colour…brown!

After his drink, Malar settled down and fell asleep.

Seamist watched him for a while, before returning to princess Shamrock.

✤✤✤

"How is he?" Shamrock asked.

"He's weak and tired, but I'm sure he'll recuperate," Seamist said with a reassuring smile.

As Seamist talked, Crystal watched her. "I don't mean to be rude," she said. "But I like the colour of your coat and your white foot? You look different to the others we've seen here."

Seamist smiled, but the sadness in her eyes deepened as she explained. "My mother was a captive rat." She looked pointedly at Shamrock. "She was brought here for my father King Flylord, but she died giving birth to us. So Liza's mother reared us. There were six of us, but only my brother and I survived."

Crystal thought for a moment and then the penny dropped.

"So you and Liza are half-sisters?"

Seamist nodded. "Sadly, my brother was killed by a fox some time ago. I really miss him."

"Oh, how awful," Shamrock said. "I have no brothers or sisters."

"I have," Crystal said. "Rather a lot!"

For a brief moment, their happy chatter and laughter helped them forget the frightening predicament they were in.

✤✤✤

In the main chamber of the den, King Flylord and his son Prince Timere listened to Zadock's report.

Hardly pausing for breath, he told them about the fight, their losses, and the successful kidnap.

Flylord's delighted grin appeared to stretch from ear to ear. "Good, good, it's a shame it has to be this way, but what else can we do, we must survive."

"I wish I had been there," Timere said.

"It was hard won," Zadock said. "But we have the Princess and Prince Malar."

"Well done Zadock. Now go and rest, I will speak with you later."

As Zadock left the chamber, Timere asked. "When can I meet the Princess, father?"

"Soon my son, but for now, we must let her rest, so be patient. I want you to join the hunting party and bring back some food," he smiled. "Tomorrow night we celebrate!"

Timere's eyes sparkled with excitement, his tail twitched. The thought of joining a hunting party and foraging for food delighted him; especially if it entailed visiting a nearby farm…he loved eggs. Though small of stature, he was brave and fast. His reputation for escaping the hungry jaws of farm dogs was legendary.

The next day, the den buzzed with activity, as preparations for the party got under way. After a successful hunt, there was plenty to eat and great excitement, as King Flylord informed everyone, that in the next few days he would present the captured Princess to his son, Prince Timere. Overjoyed at the good news, everyone celebrated the victory.

Seamist spent a lot of time with Prince Malar; she was good medicine for him. He was healing fast and gaining strength. She willingly took messages to and fro between Malar and Princess Shamrock; both had grown to trust her.

They knew their fathers would move heaven and earth to rescue them, but it would need to be soon.

Liza was becoming suspicious at the amount of time her sister was spending with Malar. She tried to tell her father, but he would hear nothing against his lovely young daughter. Frustrated, Liza vowed to keep watching them...secretly. She was sure something was going on, and she would catch them. Then, who would be daddy's favourite.

Chapter Seven

Hurrying through Windom woods, Rupert and Sky were relieved to enter King Pierro's den. Gasping for breath, Rupert fell exhausted at the King's feet.

"Take him to rest, and give him food and water," the King ordered the excited bucks standing around. "When he has recovered, I will talk with him." King Pierro turned to Sky, motioning for him to sit down. "You need to rest and eat something."

Sky thanked him and gratefully accepted the dandelion leaves set before him.

Between mouthfuls, he told the King what he knew about the violent events of the day before.

King Pierro groaned as tears filled his eyes. He could hardly believe what he was hearing. Pacing back and forth, he murmured softly. "Oh, my son, I've lost you."

Sky wished he could be of comfort, but he had no idea what to say. He told the King. "Bluebear and Loki are safe in my burrow, being cared for by my sister Cloud. I hope they will be fit to travel in a day or two."

The news pleased Pierro, as he was fond of the two old bucks. But his heart ached with worry for his son Prince Malar.

Pierro's restless pacing came to a sudden halt…a cold chill ran up his spine, as he thought of King Ludus. *He must be desperate with worry over the fate of his daughter.* Shaking his head, he said to Sky. "I must send some bucks to King Ludus, and let him know what's happened." His voice broke as he cried, "Oh my, this is a dreadful situation."

Sky politely interrupted him. "Your Highness, please let me help. Rather than send more bucks into danger, I know a wood pigeon, she is a friend. I'm sure she would be more than happy to help."

The King thought about it for a moment; when he spoke the relief was evident in his voice. "I agree, Sky. I do not wish to send more bucks into danger. But we need help and if your friend is willing, then I will be most grateful."

❦❦❦

Excusing himself from the King's presence, Sky hurried from the den, found a high point and called for his friend the pigeon. He desperately hoped she would hear him. Again and again he called, using a special high pitched sound.

To his relief a large wood pigeon flew onto a branch near the den. Landing heavily, she spent a few seconds sorting out her tail feathers.

Impatient to speak, Sky greeted her and right away began to tell her the story.

Seed was extremely laid back, her main interest in life was food, and it showed in her ample girth.

Sky first met her, when she warned him of an approaching fox, giving him time to escape. From then on their friendship blossomed. He appreciated her kind heart, and surprising wisdom.

As Sky talked, Seed gasped with shock! Her small bright eyes clouded with concern. "Oh dear, oh dear," she kept saying.

"So, can you help us?" Sky asked, quite breathless.

"Of course my dear, I will leave this minute. I am more than happy to take messages back and forth. It will be a privilege to help."

Sky thanked her and returned to the den.

Seed shouted, "I will bring word as soon as I can from King Ludus."

⚜⚜⚜

Seed flew as fast as she could; she knew the area well, so would have no trouble finding the den. She dreaded telling King Ludus the news. Having been a mother herself, many times over, she knew how he would feel. Her heart raced as she pushed herself to fly faster…desperate to reach her destination as soon as possible.

"This is a bad situation, a really bad situation," she muttered to herself. Flying through the trees, she saw the den in the distance. Perching on a branch nearby, she strutted up and down, calling loudly. Her head bobbed with agitation.

All of a sudden a large white rat appeared. "What do you want?" He asked.

"I need to see your King, my dear, and quickly. I'm afraid I have bad news. Please take me to him."

Huffing with concern, the rat scurried away and disappeared into the den. The next minute he reappeared with a number of others, following a large brown rat.

Seed realised it was the King. Lowering her head, her voice faltered as she said. "Oh, Your Highness, I'm sorry to be—"

42

Before she could continue, King Ludus said in a voice trembling with emotion. "My daughter has been taken by the wild rats, hasn't she?" He stared up at her, his brow furrowed. He knew what her answer would be.

Seed nodded. Taking a deep breath, she said in a hushed voice. "I'm sorry, but your daughter and her companion have been kidnapped by the wild rats, along with King Pierro's son, Prince Malar. We have been told Prince Malar is badly hurt. And there are many dead and injured."

"Oh my," King Ludus groaned. "I knew something was wrong, as we'd heard nothing for some time." Glancing up at Seed, he asked. "Would you come in and take some refreshment? I must speak with my council. We need a plan of action."

Seed agreed and followed him to the entrance of the den. She waited patiently, guessing there would be a message to take to King Pierro.

This situation could keep me busy for some time, she thought. *Still, with all this flying to and fro, I will lose some weight, and be of help at the same time.* Her eyes brightened as she tucked into the tasty corn the rats brought her.

Deep in the den, King Ludus and his council were struggling to come up with a rescue plan.

As Seed finished her corn, an idea popped into her head. Strutting to the dens entrance, she called out, "I would like to see the King."

A big grey rat lumbered towards her. In a voice like gravel he said. "The King is busy. As you know he is formulating a plan to rescue his daughter."

Seed's head bobbed with excitement. "I know, and I have an idea I would like to put to him. Please, fetch him, do not delay."

The urgency in her voice spurred the rat. Darkness cloaked him, as he disappeared deeper into the den.

Seed tapped her foot as she waited by the entrance. Hearing the sound of scurrying feet, she stood to attention. Seeing the King appear out of the darkness, she cried. "Your Highness, I apologise for disturbing you, but I have an idea. There is a way to rescue the captives without more violence. I know someone who can help us." Seeing she had the King's attention, her pounding heart slowed. "His name is Optimus, your highness. He is an owl…old and wise. He lives in the forest of Grendeen; but it won't take me long to reach him."

Pausing, she gazed at the eager faces staring at her. Her voice rose with confidence as she explained. "Optimus has knowledge of this whole area. He knows everything and everyone. If anyone can help us, he can!" Seed stared earnestly at the King, hoping he would allow her to help.

King Ludus clenched his teeth, his long tail twitched. *Can I trust an owl?* He sighed. *What choice do I have? Time is of th*e *essence.* Staring into Seed's dark eyes, he rose on his back legs; his voice quivered as he said, "Very well, go to him. But I trust you will make him understand the urgency of this situation?" Tilting his head to the side, he studied her.

Seed returned his gaze; her heart ached. In a voice choked with emotion, she softly said. "Trust me your Highness. I promise I won't let you down." Rising into the air she cried. "I will be in touch soon."

Chapter Eight

It was a beautiful evening. The suns fading light bathed the sky in soft hues of gold and orange. Seed flew towards her destination, the distant forest. Behind her, night cloaked the landscape in darkness…ahead the last glimmers of daylight drew her on.

Seed smiled. *How poetic. Behind is darkness and trouble; ahead there is light, and hopefully an answer to this bad situation.*

For a brief moment, Seed felt an uncomfortable tightness in her chest. The thought Optimus might not be willing to help, had not occurred to her. "Goodness," she tutted attempting to maintain confidence. "Don't be silly, of course he will."

She reached the edge of the forest as the sun disappeared below the horizon. It was dark and eerie among the trees. Peering into the shadows, Seed weaved and turned to avoid low branches. Eventually she came to a clearing, with a large ancient oak standing proudly in the centre.

Perching on a branch, Seed called softly, desperately hoping the great owl was at home. She continued to coo and flap her wings, until she heard movement from inside the tree. A large flat head with huge staring eyes appeared from deep inside the trunk.

"Who is making all that noise?" The owl demanded.

Seed's tongue stuck to the roof of her beak. Swallowing hard she flew to a branch near him and asked. "Excuse me for disturbing you, but are you Optimus the wise?"

His huge eyes increased in size as he stared at her. "I am. Who wants to know?" His deep voice was resonant and authoritative.

Taking a deep breath, Seed told him her name, and proceeded to tell him about the rats' dilemma. When she finished, she was quite breathless. Tilting her head, she gazed at Optimus. His silence and intense expression unnerved her.

Hissing softly, Optimus said. "You have not told me anything I don't already know. I've been waiting for such a time as this." Fluffing his feathers, he rotated his head almost full circle.

Seed drew back, her eyes wide.

"I believe I have the answer the Kings are looking for, but it won't be easy." His eyes narrowed, as he stared thoughtfully into the distance. In a voice strangely quiet, he said to Seed. "I will require a volunteer; one who is more than brave." Optimus fixed his hypnotic stare upon Seed, his eyes unblinking.

Seed trembled in his unwavering gaze. *Gosh, I hope he doesn't mean me.* Before she could say anything, he spread his wings and told her to follow him. Launching off the branch, Seed flapped frantically in her effort to keep up with him. Gasping for breath, she grumbled. "All this flying to and fro is exhausting." As they soared over the forest, she realised they were flying back to King Ludus.

Arriving at the rats den, Optimus alighted gracefully near the entrance.

Seed arrived and crash landed beside him, exhausted and gasping for breath.

"You need to get fit," he said.

"Tell me something I don't know," she replied. Seeing the flicker of a smile in his eyes she tutted at him.

Ignoring her, Optimus called to the inhabitants of the den.

King Ludus arrived, closely followed by a number of his bucks; all were tense and trembling. Under normal conditions, rats were dinner for an owl, but this was not normal, and Optimus was not your average owl.

Talking softly to them, he quickly gained their confidence. "Have you heard of the Rat Run?" He asked. Their reaction was all the answer he needed. From King Ludus down, every rat shook with fear.

Cocking her head to the side, Seed frowned. *Why are they all so afraid?* She stared at Optimus. "What's the Rat Run and why is everyone so scared?"

Raising a brow, Optimus glanced at King Ludus.

"Tell her," Ludus said. "She's helping us, so has earned the right to know."

"Very well," Optimus turned to Seed and told her about the Rat Run.

Seed's heart pounded as she listened. Like the rats an involuntary tremble shook her body.

"The Rat Run is a hard surface, so wide you can hardly see the grass in the middle." Optimus explained. "If one survives the hard surface and reaches the grass in the middle, they are safe. However, they cannot stay there. They must cross the second hard surface to the land beyond. And again the barrier to the land beyond is the huge roaring monsters. They own the hard surface and kill any creature that gets in their way."

Seed's beak dropped open. She stood speechless, now she understood why the rats were so afraid. In a tremulous voice, she asked. "But what is so important about the land beyond?"

Taking a deep breath, Optimus said. "The land beyond, is where the answer can be found for the disputes and constant fighting that goes on between the fancy rats and the wild rats."

Seed's eyes narrowed as she stared at him. "What's a fancy rat?"

Hissing with impatience, he explained. "Fancy rats are those who've had contact with humans, like King Ludus, and King Pierro." Raising a wing, he gestured at the rats gathered round. "You see the variety of colour among the bucks here?"

Seed nodded.

"Well, as you know, the wild rats are all the same colour. Not only that, they are hated by everyone, particularly humans. Obviously, they don't like that, hence they try to unite with fancy rats, to improve themselves and find acceptance."

Seed thought for a moment. "So you're saying the wild rats suffer prejudice."

"Exactly," Optimus said. "But not just because of their colour you understand. They have deep seated issues, which need to be dealt with. Until this problem is solved, there will always be trouble. Not all the wild rats are bad, and not all the fancy rats are good," Glancing at Ludus, he smiled. "Present company excepted of course."

Having enlightened Seed, they continued to discuss the problem at hand. Optimus explained, the one chosen to cross the hard surface to the land beyond, will find the great Oracle.

"The one who goes must understand the Oracle is a living being." Lowering his head, Optimus narrowed his eyes at them. "They must approach with respect. He is ancient, and cannot be hurried."

Rising to his full height, Optimus stared at the trembling rats. "The sooner someone is found the better. The one who goes must volunteer freely. He will go alone, no one can help him. There will be witnesses to watch him cross to the land beyond and return. They will be the three Kings involved in this dispute." Glancing at Ludus, he asked. "Do you agree to this?"

King Ludus nodded. "I do, but I can't speak for the others."

"Very well, I will dispatch message birds to King Pierro, and King Flylord, informing them of our plan. I'll invite them to join us here, as this is the nearest point to the Rat Run. Once everyone is here, a volunteer will be found from among you. We can only hope and pray they succeed."

Chapter Nine

Back at King Flylord's Den, Liza and Timere sat grooming each other. Timere noticed how quiet she was, not her usual self at all.

"What's wrong?" he asked

Lowering her eyes, Liza murmured. "I wish father liked me, as much as he likes you and Seamist."

Timere sat back in surprise. "Of course he likes you. Where did you get that idea from? I bet this is because Seamist and that buck Prince Malar, like each other, and I am to have the Princess Shamrock."

Liza didn't answer. She huffed and stared at the ground.

Timere gently groomed her behind the ears, knowing she particularly enjoyed it.

Liza relaxed and ground her teeth with appreciation.

"There will be someone for you soon, you'll see," Timere said.

Liza made no comment. How could she tell him she liked Zadock; it had to be her secret. To her surprise, Zadock appeared, agitated and in a great hurry.

"The King wants you both in his chamber, now!"

They followed him, curious to know what their father could want so urgently.

In the main chamber of the den, the King stood surrounded by most of the residents. The air sparked with united anxiety.

A large black rook, stood alongside the King, its expression serious.

Timere and Liza huddled together, their hearts racing as they gazed at the strange scene.

Seamist hurried in and joined them. In a hushed voice she asked. "What's going on?"

"We don't know," Liza whispered.

Spotting them among the large crowd of rats, the King called them to join him.

Fidgeting…tails twitching, the three youngsters kept a wary eye on the rook, as they stood beside their father.

When everyone was quiet, King Flylord raised his voice and relayed the message brought by the rook. In a voice strangely shaky, he said. "This night, I am going to the den of King Ludus. This rook and one volunteer will accompany me. A plan has been formulated, which if successful, will unite all rats once and for all."

A great murmur went up from among the assembly.

Raising his head, the King took a deep breath and continued. "The volunteer, along with two others from King Ludus and King Pierro's clans, will each draw straws. The one who gets the short straw must do the Rat Run."

Horrified cries filled the chamber. The corporate fear was tangible. Who would volunteer? Silence filled the chamber. You could cut the atmosphere with a knife. Everyone knew about the Rat Run, it brought fear to them all, even the bravest, even Zadock! Rats stared at their neighbours. Others attempted to back unnoticed out of the chamber.

In the growing chaos, a squeaky voice was heard. It came from close to the King. It was Timere.

"I will go," he said.

Shocked! Flylord stared at his son, and cried. "No! Not you!" He saw the rook looking at him and dropped his head. His legs trembled…threatened to give way beneath him. The rules clearly stated, the first one to volunteer whoever it was, must be accepted.

"Timere, what are you doing?" Liza and Seamist cried.

Timere's voice faltered as he said. "It'll be alright, don't worry."

Liza glared at him; in a voice high pitched with emotion, she squeaked. "It won't be alright." Tears trickled down her cheeks.

"What if you pick the short straw?" Seamist said nuzzling his neck.

Before Timere could answer her, the King's voice silenced them. "Quiet!" He shouted. "Prince Timere has volunteered. He must be accepted, it is the law. We leave now with the rook. Zadock will accompany us. Nothing must be done until I return."

Nothing more was said. The massed body of rats parted, allowing the King, the rook, Prince Timere and Zadock to walk through their midst. The stunned rodents followed them to the den's entrance.

For a brief moment, Prince Timere paused and glanced back at Liza and Seamist.

His smile gave them little encouragement as they watched him vanish into the night.

The rook flew low to lead and give protection. They moved as fast, and as silently as possible. Darkness quickly swallowed them; hiding them from the view of all at the den.

෯෯෯

Meanwhile, back in the meadow, safe in the rabbits care, Bluebear and Loki were recovering well. Sadly, Captain succumbed to infection from his broken leg and passed away.

The rabbits buried him under an old oak tree. As Bluebear and Loki sat close by paying their respects, a sparrow perched on a branch above their heads.

"Are you from King Pierro's den?" he asked.

The two old warriors nodded.

"He needs you to return as soon as possible," the sparrow said.

Bluebear and Loki listened in amazement, as he shared the news. When the word Rat Run was mentioned, the two old warriors huddled together huffing in fear.

The little sparrow stared sympathetically at them. "I know you are afraid, but your King needs you. You must leave right away, it will be dark soon."

Bluebear nodded, rising to his feet, he told the sparrow to fly back and tell King Pierro they were returning home.

"Hurry," the sparrow called as he flew away.

Cloud could feel their tension as she led them back to the burrow. The other rabbits followed at a distance. The sparrow's news had surprised them all, filling them with dread. All animals, especially the rabbits were aware of the Rat Run…they feared it. In a sympathetic voice, Cloud asked. "Will you be leaving now?"

"Yes," Loki said. "Can you show us the tunnel Sky used to take Rupert home?"

"Of course I can." Leading them into the burrow, cloud turned into a dark tunnel. "This way is faster than going around the meadow," she said.

Bluebear and Loki followed her into the darkness. Moving fast they eventually saw a light up ahead.

Running out of the tunnel, Cloud led them to the safety of a thick bush. "This is where I must leave you," she told them.

"How can we thank you for all you've done for us?"

"It has been our pleasure," Cloud said. "Will you find your way from here?"

Bluebear smiled and assured her they would be fine. Bowing low, he and Loki thanked her.

Raising a paw, Cloud brushed away a tear as she watched them vanish in the undergrowth. "Stay safe," she whispered, before returning to the tunnel.

Bluebear led the way. As darkness fell, they arrived at the edge of Squirrel territory. In the distance they could see Windom woods.

"Nearly there," Bluebear said. Pausing for breath, he sat for a moment.

"We should keep going," Loki said. "We don't want to alert the squirrels to our presence."

Breathing hard, Bluebear told him to lead the way. "Mind that piece of open ground," he warned.

Running as fast as they could, they dodged from cover to cover, until at last they reached the woods. Their racing hearts calmed when they saw the den ahead of them.

Bluebear spotted Rupert and Sky the rabbit foraging at the dens entrance, he gasped with relief. It was a welcome sight.

Raising his head, Rupert saw them first. Squeaking with delight, he ran to greet them.

Sky joined in the excited welcome. "How is everyone at my burrow?" he asked.

Bluebear and Loki assured him all was well. Chatting happily, they hurried into the safety of the den.

Chapter Ten

King Pierro, hearing the noise came to investigate. Seeing Bluebear and Loki, his eyes shone with delight. "Welcome back," he cried. "The sparrow told us you were making your way home. I'm so glad you're safe and well." Glancing round he whispered. "Come to my chamber, I have much to tell you."

Bluebear and Loki followed him into his private chamber. Once they were alone, Bluebear noticed King Pierro's countenance change…the worry in his ruby eyes.

"Your Highness, is there any news about Prince Malar, or Princess Shamrock?"

Pierro sighed and shook his head. "No, Bluebear. But I'm hoping there may be a solution to the problem, even if a dangerous one."

"Do you mean the Rat Run?" Loki asked.

Pierro visibly trembled. "I'm afraid so. Optimus the owl has devised a plan, which if it works, will unite us all. However, there is no guarantee of success and it is fraught with danger." Frowning, King Pierro rose to his feet. "Do you think you can make another journey so soon? It will be dangerous, but a rook has been sent to accompany us." Raising a brow, he studied them.

Swishing his long tail, Bluebear glanced at Loki. The big rat smiled and said confidently. "Don't be concerned, Your Highness. We are well."

"Good," the King said with a relieved sigh. "In a few moments we leave to go to King Ludus. King Flylord is already on his way there."

At the mention of Flylord's name, Bluebear and Loki bristled with anger, their tails twitched.

Seeing their agitated state…their fluffed fur, King Pierro said calmly. "We must try to resolve this unpleasantness; and grasp the opportunity to unite with those we consider our enemy." Staring at them, his eyes narrowed as he said softly. "I won't force either of you to come, but the black rook is waiting for us."

"Lead on," Bluebear said. No way would he let his King go without him.

Loki nodded in agreement. "Who else will accompany us?" He asked.

King Pierro sighed. "Prince Piper insists on coming with us."

Bluebear and Loki exchanged a worried glance.

Sitting on his haunches, the King raised his paws. "I've tried to talk him out of it, but without success, I'm afraid. He wants to help his brother Malar."

"Understandable, I suppose," Bluebear muttered.

The King grimaced as he told them Princess Pecan wanted to come as well.

Loki's eyes widened as he exclaimed. "Oh no, I hope you—"

"She is staying here," Pierro quickly interjected. "Rupert and aunty Freckle will look after her. Although I have to say, she is not happy. There have been tears and tantrums."

"Better that, than going into danger," Bluebear said.

Nodding with agreement, Pierro led them to the dens entrance, where Piper waited with the rook.

Smiling with delight, he greeted the two old warriors. But with no time to spare, they formed a tight group and hurried after the rook.

They each knew the journey would not be easy, or pleasant. They had plenty to think about as they followed the rook.

The bird's sharp eyes were peeled for danger. If he saw or heard anything suspicious, he would perch, and allow the rats to scurry under cover. With so much stopping and starting, the journey took a while. But at last, exhausted and breathing hard, they entered the den of King Ludus.

The den heaved with extra bodies. The tense atmosphere…amplified by King Flylord's intimidating presence, added to the general air of anxiety. The thought of the Rat Run weighed heavy on them all. Once the awkward greetings were over, they followed King Ludus into a large chamber.

Optimus the owl, was already there waiting for them.

Silently, they gathered in family groups. King Pierro, with Piper, Bluebear and Loki, stood on one side of the chamber.

King Flylord with his son Prince Timere and Zadock crouched in a corner on the other side. While King Ludus with a trusted buck beside him, stood his ground in the middle. All eyes were glued to Optimus.

The great owl rose to his full height; he cut an imposing figure as he stretched out his wings, to make sure he had their undivided attention. "You all know why we have gathered here," he said. Looking around the packed chamber, he asked. "Do we have any volunteers?"

"Yes sir," Prince Timere said, trying to stop his voice from trembling. "I volunteer for my father and my clan,"

"Very well, you are accepted," Optimus said.

Piper turned to King Pierro. "I will go for us father." Before a word could be said, he was up and standing beside Timere.

King Pierro made to follow and bring him back, but a look from Optimus froze him to the spot.

Glancing at Piper, Optimus said. "You are accepted." Facing King Ludus, he raised his voice. "Who will volunteer for King Ludus, he has no son to represent him?"

To everyone's amazement, Bluebear joined the two youngsters.

"Accepted," Optimus said. "Now, one of you must be chosen to do the Rat Run, we will use straws to do this. The one who draws the short straw will go."

The three of them trembled, as an old white rat from King Ludus's clan, waddled towards them. In his paw he held three straws their length concealed.

Prince Timere chose first. Looking at it he frowned.

Bluebear chose next, holding the straw close to his chest.

Prince Piper took the remaining straw.

Holding their straws up for Optimus to check, it was obvious Prince Timere had the shortest straw.

Fisting his paws, King Flylord gasped for breath. Nevertheless, he knew the decision was final; his son must go. The future for peace and harmony now rested upon Prince Timere. He alone had the opportunity to bring lasting peace and unity to all rats.

Optimus ordered everyone, apart from the three Kings and Prince Timere to leave the chamber. In a sombre tone, he commended Timere for his bravery, before commanding the small party to follow him.

Without further ceremony, they began their journey to the hard surface.

Optimus warned them; not only was the Rat Run extremely dangerous, but so was the journey to get there.

Due to thick clouds, it was a particularly dark night; neither the moon, nor the stars were visible. All around the air was filled with nocturnal noise. The little party stayed as close together as possible, their ears twitching to every sound.

Optimus glided among the trees, staying as close as he could, without coming to grief because of low branches. He needed to be ahead of them, but at the same time keep them in sight; as he was the only one who knew how to get there.

The rats struggled through the long grass, finding whatever cover they could. Suddenly, another owl flew overhead and spotted them, but before it had a chance to attack, Optimus sternly warned it off.

Protesting loudly, the owl flew into a tree.

"Keep going!" Optimus shouted at the rats. "It's not far now."

Encouraged, they moved on again following his lead. Ahead they could see the dark outline of a wood. Beyond it was the hard surface. In fact, occasionally they heard a distant roar; which did little for Prince Timere's confidence.

Struggling on, they entered the relative safety of the woods…darkness covered them like a comfy blanket. Timere wished he could stay there and hide.

He trembled at the thought of what lay ahead. His coat fluffed with agitation. His heart drummed in his ears, but he knew he had to go on. Struggling with his fears, he was taken by surprise when everyone stopped.

Two large forms had appeared in front of them, as if from nowhere. Their small dark eyes glistened with evil intent. Their sharp white teeth flashed like daggers in the darkness.

"What are you doing in our woodsss?" one of them hissed.

"Yesss get out of our woodsss." the other one snarled.

Their pronounced lisp, accentuated the evil sound of their voices. Creeping closer, hunger glinted in the creatures piggy eyes.

The little group of rats scuttled back and huddled together for protection. Frantically, they looked around for Optimus, but he was nowhere to be seen.

They realized these two nasty individuals were mink, possibly escapees from a local mink farm. This meant unless Optimus was near, they were in big trouble.

Mink were hated, and known by all for their cruelty. They would kill anything, and sometimes just for fun. These two large males had their sights set on the rats.

As the small group prepared to defend itself, a soft wind blew over them, ruffling their fur. In an instant they knew it was Optimus, and breathed sighs of relief.

Optimus descended on the mink, his huge talons outstretched.

They took one look and fled.

He pursued them a short way, just to make sure they got the message, before returning to the frightened rats. "Are you alright?" He asked.

Huddled together and breathing hard, they nodded.

"Good, let's go, we're nearly there now."

The gentleness in his voice soothed them. His presence filled them with renewed confidence. They followed him, running as fast as they could.

Optimus stayed as close as possible as he led them on the last leg of the journey.

Prince Timere struggled with his thoughts. *One danger may be past, but what will I have to face next?*

As they drew closer to the hard surface, they could hear the monsters roar...see their yellow eyes flashing through the trees. The ground shook as each monster thundered past.

Timere trembled, his legs wobbled like jelly. Instinct urged him to flatten himself to the ground and hide, but he knew his father and the others were relying on him. Sucking in air, he summoned every ounce of courage and kept going.

Under a bush at the edge of the hard surface, Optimus waited for them.

Quietly, he told Timere what he must do...tried to impress upon him the dangers of the Rat Run. To reinforce his message, he fixed his large hypnotic eyes on the young Prince. Feeling he'd made his point he continued. "Whatever you do, don't hurry to get across the hard surface. Watch and listen. However long you take, we will be waiting here. When you reach the other side you will see a tall barrier made of wood. Search close to the ground, you will find a hole, crawl through it and find the Oracle."

Gazing into Timere's terrified face, he said softly. "In the Oracle's presence, be patient and humble; listen carefully. What he tells you will change things for ever, for all of you." Glancing at the three Kings huddled under the hedge, he said to Timere, "When the Oracle is finished, you must cross the hard surface and return to us. Do you understand?"

Timere nodded, so frightened he could hardly breathe, never mind speak. His tongue stuck to the roof of his mouth.

Optimus and the others moved back into the bushes, leaving Timere and King Flylord alone for a moment to say their goodbyes. The two of them huddled together.

Flylord kissed his son; his voice trembled as he said with uncharacteristic gentleness. "I'm proud of you my boy; be brave, do your best and whatever happens, I will always remember your courage; we all will."

Unable to speak, Prince Timere nestled close to his father, comforted by his warmth and strength.

Optimus returned. The great owl fixed Timere with his hypnotic stare. "As I said before young Prince, don't rush across the hard surface, watch the monsters eyes and try to judge the distance. That's all the help I can give you. Don't let fear defeat you. The fact you have been chosen, means you are special...remember that. Now go; we will be here when you return."

Swallowing hard, Timere turned away from the comforting presence of his father and the other Kings; their worried expressions added to his misery. Slowly, on shaky legs he made his way through thick shrubbery towards the hard surface and crouched in the long grass at the edge.

Chapter Eleven

Afraid to move, Timere cowered there for some time, comforted by the surrounding darkness. Whenever a monster roared past, he would gasp and flatten his body in the grass. Some of them had such huge feet; the ground shook as they thundered by. Their hard yellow eyes glared at him.

Shaking and temporarily blinded, Timere whimpered and closed his eyes. Some of the monsters screamed at him, while others made a deep growling noise. He held on to the grass with his paws…afraid he would be blown away in the force of the wind their huge bodies created.

Everything in him cried. *Run back to the others, don't go*! But he knew he couldn't. They were relying on him. Digging deep, he found the courage he needed. He remembered Optimus's advice, to watch the monsters eyes and judge the distance between them.

Pulling himself together, Timere looked to where the monsters were coming from. He noticed the frequency of their approach had diminished. Raising his head he stared at the hard surface. *I wonder where all the monsters are going*? Shaking his head, he thought. *They sound furious and are obviously in a great hurry*. His brow furrowed as he struggled to understand.

Peering into the darkness; he couldn't see a thing. His body tingled in the eerie silence. *It's now or never*, he thought. With his eyes glued to the grass in the centre of the hard surface, he made a dash for it. Just in time, he reached it, as a monster raced past. The angry scream deafened him...the wind its body created nearly blew him over.

Crouched in a clump of grass, Timere's lungs burned as he struggled to get his breath. Resting his head on his paws, he waited for his racing heart to slow.

Lying there in the cool grass, he noticed it seemed quieter on the second hard surface. One monster raced towards him, its voice a dull roar. But behind the monster, there was nothing but darkness. No more yellow eyes could be seen approaching.

When the monster passed, Timere sneaked out and scuttled as fast as he could to the other side. Collapsing under a large bush, he lay there exhausted...more from fear than exertion. He was aware, not only were there monsters to fear, there were also night predators. Being a rodent, his eyesight was poor. He squinted in an effort to see. However, his acute hearing missed nothing, his small pink ears twitched to every sound.

Gradually, Timere's rapid breathing slowed and he felt able to move. Creeping out from under the bush, he made his way across a piece of open ground. Ahead, he saw the tall wooden barrier mentioned by Optimus; it blocked his path.

Scurrying along the bottom of the barrier, Timere found a small hole. He crawled through, and found himself in a large enclosed space. Hunkering down, he was grateful for the darkness, hiding him from view.

It was too dark to see much, but his ears twitched to a strange sound coming from his right. Straining to see, Timere blinked. He could just make out a large rock, with a strange pattern on it. Creeping closer, he cringed, the hair rose on the back of his neck. Huffing with fear, his eyes widened in disbelief...sticking out of the rock were thick scaly legs with long claws.

To make matters worse, the rock moved. Using its strange legs, it turned towards him; a large scaly head with small beady eyes emerged from inside the rock and stared at him.

With a frightened squeak, Timere flattened his body to the ground. Narrowing his eyes, his long tail twitched, as he bravely prepared to defend himself. Holding his breath, he hoped the strange creature couldn't see him. However, his hope was dashed, as the stone spoke.

With a terrified gasp, Timere leapt back.

The stone's voice was surprisingly soft, as it asked. "Who are you, and what do you want?"

Shaking uncontrollably, Timere raised his head and in a choked voice said. "Please, don't hurt me. I am looking for the Oracle, we need his help." In the brief silence, Timere took a few calming breaths.

"I am the Oracle," the rock said moving closer. "Who needs my help?"

The kindness in the Oracle's voice gave Timere confidence. Settling in the grass, he told the Oracle the whole story. Told him how his clan, the wild rats, always felt hated by the fancy rats. He tried to explain why his father King Flylord, would send out bucks to kidnap the other rats females. "We want to be more like them. But it doesn't work...nothing changes. In fact things are getting worse." Sighing, he played with the grass, pulling at it with his paws.

Saying nothing, the Oracle watched him.

Raising his head, Timere returned the Oracle's gaze. His voice faltered as he told him about the fighting...the deaths and injuries on both sides. "We all want it to stop. Optimus the wise owl is helping us. He said you would have the answer."

Noting the Oracle's quizzical expression, Timere's heart fell. Nevertheless, he carried on talking, in the hope the Oracle would be moved to assist them. "Three of us volunteered to do the Rat Run, and come here to you. I drew the short straw."

Raising a paw, Timere rubbed his eye and leaned towards the Oracle. In a voice tinged with anger, he said. "Doing the Rat Run, has been the worst experience of my life! I did it for the sake of peace…for unity. Optimus said you could help us." Timere stopped for a moment to catch his breath. "Please, don't let my sacrifice be a waste," he pleaded. "Will you help us?"

The Oracle remained silent, he didn't move. In fact his head disappeared inside the stone, only his nose could be seen.

Unsure what to do, Timere sat still, trying to be patient as instructed by Optimus.

Suddenly, the Oracle spoke. "Come here," it commanded.

Holding his breath, Timere crept closer.

The scaly head came out of the rock and peered at him. There was a brief pause, before the Oracle asked Timere. "How do you feel about the fancy rats?"

Timere's eyes flashed. "We hate them," he replied.

With a stern edge to his voice, the Oracle said. "I asked what you personally feel, not your clan."

Taken by surprise, Timere took a moment to think. Being asked his opinion about anything was a new experience. He needed to give the question serious consideration. Scratching behind his ear, he stared at the Oracle. "To be honest, I've never given much thought to how I personally feel about the fancy rats. Like everyone else, I just accepted the situation. It's how it is…part of life."

However, as Timere sat there and pondered the question, to his amazement, he realised he didn't hate the fancy rats at all. His anger towards them was fuelled by his father and the other rats.

Staring at him, the Oracle waited patiently for an answer.

Gazing into the Oracle's eyes, Timere was shocked to hear his own voice say. "No, I don't hate them. In fact, I wish we could all get on and be friends." Sitting up, he smiled and said. "Take my sister Seamist for example. She's made friends with the Prince we captured from one of the fancy clans. She spends a lot of time looking after him, as he was injured when my father's bucks stole their Princess. In the battle, many rats from all sides were killed or injured." Seeing the Oracle's serious expression, Timere lowered his head and crouched in the grass.

"So, are you telling me you want friendship and peace with the fancy rats?" The Oracle asked.

Raising his head, Timere exclaimed. "Oh yes. I'm sure we all do really, if we are honest."

Stretching his large scaly head towards Timere, the Oracle fixed him with a hypnotic stare.

The young prince sat quietly, amazed how calm he felt in the presence of this imposing creature.

In a gentle voice, the Oracle said. "The fact you've had the courage to do the Rat Run, and come here, shows me you are sincere. It is right you were chosen. I will help you, but you must follow my advice. It will not be easy, do you think you can?"

Timere nodded. His voice faltered as he said softly. "I will try."

Tilting his head the Oracle studied Timere. When he continued, his expression was serious. "To do the Rat Run is hard enough...to follow my advice and live by it, is even harder. You must search inside yourself for hidden depths of character. It is there you must find it. As you seek to do what is right, with courage and integrity. Your character will show itself and grow. Then and only then, will you become the leader and King you are destined to be."

Gazing at the Oracle...hearing his words, Timere could feel his heart flutter. He had never seen himself as a leader, and certainly not a King. And yet as he thought about it, he realised he was his father's only son, there was no one else. He was the prince, and thus heir to his father's Kingdom.

Timere looked up at the Oracle, deep inside he knew things had to change. Fighting and stealing had achieved nothing, only mutual hatred and mistrust. Lowering his head, Timere assured the Oracle, he would do his best to be a good King and leader.

The Oracle's scaly face softened in a smile. Lowering his rock-like body to the ground, he drew in his legs, until only his head showed. Stretching his long neck, he fixed his dark round eyes on Timere, and began to tell him about a book…a book so old it had been around since the beginning of time.

"This ancient book is filled with wise teachings," the Oracle said in a voice thick with reverence. "I have spent most of my life studying it and learning to follow its precepts." Closing his eyes, his voice dropped to a whisper. "The writings in this book have blessed me with wisdom and long life."

Timere listened intently as the Oracle spoke.

"Many, like yourself young Prince, have risked the dangerous journey to come and see me."

Tilting his head to the side, Timere asked. "Did they follow your advice? Were they successful?"

Opening his eyes, the Oracle blew through his nose.

To avoid a shower, Timere jumped back.

"I have no idea as to the outcome of their visit. Suffice to say, I gave them the same advice, I'm giving you." The Oracle's eyes narrowed as he said. "Fighting, young Prince achieves nothing. In fact violence results in more violence. It's like the ripples in a pond when a stone is thrown. They go on and on affecting more and more lives." Shaking his head, he continued softly.

"Vengeance is a whirlwind. It wreaks havoc, devastating lives and leaving sorrow and grief in its wake. It is a cycle with no end." Pausing, he stretched his amazingly long neck and stared long and hard at Timere. "That is, until someone breaks the cycle and that someone is you! If you are to have the peace you desire, then you must all learn to live together."

"But how can we?" Timere asked. "They hate us!"

"They don't hate you. They suffer the same affliction as you...fear and mistrust."

Sitting on his haunches, Timere sighed and raised his paws. His voice broke as he asked. "What can I do about it?"

"You must return the captives to their fathers. And be sure to keep the lines of communication open. Talking is the best way to diffuse a difficult situation. As you communicate with each other, trust will grow." Seeing Timere's dubious expression his eyes narrowed.

"You, my boy, will take the lead in this...be the go between, the one who keeps the peace. A great responsibility is on your young shoulders. Success or failure depends on how you respond in a given situation. When you are treated with suspicion, you must show you can be trusted. If you are attacked, don't fight back, show respect at all times. Cultivate kindness."

Timere twitched his tail and frowned. "I don't know if I can do what you say, and I'm not sure I fully—"

Knowing Timere's thoughts, his confusion, the Oracle was quick to explain.

"Kindness is treating others, in the way you would like to be treated and doing it without an ulterior motive. You start among your own clan, from your father down. As their leader, in time they will follow your example. The fancy rats will see the difference, and begin to trust you. Gradually, the situation will improve." His dark eyes studied Timere.

"I know you are thinking, why should we be the ones to change? It's the fancy rats that hate us, and keep their distance from us. However, this is the way it must be. You are the ones who have caused most of the trouble, and shown yourselves to be wild and unfriendly. Is this not true?" he asked.

Lowering his head, Timere nodded.

"Then it is you and yours, who must begin to put things right. You must show the others; underneath there is no difference between you. A rat is a rat, no matter what colour. Under the skin, you are the same animal."

Timere's heart fluttered, his confidence grew as he listened to the Oracle. *I wish I could stay here with him. There is so much I could learn.* Timere had never heard words like these before. The Oracle's teaching was radical, yet felt right. He wished he could stay and not return to his father and the other Kings. But dawn was approaching; soon the birds would be awake and singing…soon he would be forced to face the hard surface and the angry monsters.

"Don't worry about the coming dawn," the Oracle said. "There are fewer monsters abroad at this time, so it will be safer for you."

Timere sighed with relief, "That's good to hear." Relaxing in the grass, Timere stared at the Oracle, *how did he know what I was thinking?*

Ignoring Timere's quizzical expression, the Oracle asked. "Have you understood what I've said?"

"Yes," Timere said, with a thoughtful nod. "But how will I convince my father, and the others. How will I make them understand?"

"It won't be easy. For you are the smallest and considered the weakest of your father's children. Nevertheless, in you is great strength, which has nothing to do with your size. You are the one they will watch and follow. Your heart is good, young Prince. Dig deep, find the courage buried within you. You have everything you need…every word I have spoken you will remember."

The Oracles legs slowly emerged from inside the stone. Rising a few inches from the ground, he plodded closer to Timere.

Timere stood and bowed his head.

Lowering his mighty head, the Oracle gazed at Timere. "Look at me," he said gently.

Timere raised his head. The Oracle was so close he could smell the grass on his breath.

"Before you leave, young Prince, your name must be changed. No longer are you Timere, the timid one. From this day forward you will be called Soar, which means to rise, to fly upwards."

Timere gasped, he could feel hot tears prick at the back of his eyes. He squeezed them shut, knowing if he blinked, the tears would flow. In a voice choked with emotion, he said. "Thank you. I will try to be all you have said I can be, and do all you have told me to do."

The Oracle nodded, his bright round eyes softened in a smile. "Oh, you will my boy, you will. Now go in peace and may the wisdom of the great book be with you."

Chapter Twelve

Returning to the hole in the fence, Soar's head reeled with all the strange and wonderful things the Oracle had told him. Smiling to himself, he kept repeating his new name, Soar, over and over again. *Strange*, he thought. *It feels right, as though it's always been my name.* His heart raced with excitement, so much so, he had to take a calming breath, as the hard surface was just ahead. Settling in a clump of grass, he readied himself for the dash across to the other side.

In the distance, he could see the sun rising above the trees. It bathed the woods in a soft glow, which beckoned to him. *This is where you belong*, it seemed to say. Soar knew it was true, even though he wanted to stay with the Oracle…on the other side of the hard surface was his home. His father and his clan were waiting for him.

Above his head, two blackbirds were arguing. The rustling leaves, and the raucous cries of the birds, disturbed Soar. Huffing, he glanced up at them, before scuttling closer to the hard surface. Crouched at the edge, he breathed a sigh of relief. The Oracle was right, there seemed to be fewer monsters. Apart from the birds it was strangely silent.

Relying more on his ears than his eyes, Soar could hear nothing approaching; as far as he could see all was clear. So, taking a deep breath, he made a mad dash for the grass in the centre. The other side of the hard surface seemed equally quiet. But as Soar prepared to move, one bright eye appeared in the distance. It raced towards him.

The monster's mighty roar shattered the early morning silence. Burying his head in the grass, Soar held his breath and played dead. Raising one eyelid, he watched the one eyed monster approach; its enraged scream deafened him. As the huge monster roared past, the sound vibrated painfully through Soar's small body.

In the monster's wake, a violent gust of wind whipped through his fur, chilling him to the bone. Shivering, he huddled in the long grass. He feared this monster more than those with two eyes. *Maybe it's angry, because it only has one eye*, he thought. Taking a deep breath, he pulled himself together and checked the hard surface again; all seemed quiet…not a monster in sight.

Leaping out of the grass, Soar ran as fast as his trembling legs would carry him. Keeping his eyes focused on the woods ahead of him. He listened to the rhythmic tapping of his nails on the hard surface. His long tail swished from side to side, propelling him forward. By the time he reached the other side, he was gasping for breath and shaking.

Struggling through thick foliage, he cowed under the roots of a large tree. Desperate to join his father and the others, he called out and waited…no reply. His heart sank. Soar groaned as an uncomfortable tightness gripped his chest. *They wouldn't leave me, I know they wouldn't. Maybe they didn't hear me.* Crawling from his hiding place, he called again. Spurred by fear, the level of his voice rose. Hoping they'd heard him, he backed under the tree roots, and waited.

Soar quietly exhaled, as his father's voice drifted towards him. Relief washed over him; adrenalin strengthened his tired legs. Hearing the soft whoosh of wings, he peered out.

Optimus touched down and greeted him. "Welcome back young Prince. Thank the heavens you are safe."

Leaving his hiding place, Soar stared up at Optimus. He could see respect in the owl's large eyes.

With a bowed head, Optimus said. "Come, follow me, I will escort you to your father." Unsure how to respond, Soar's mouth gaped, his eyes widened as he followed Optimus.

King Flylord and the other Kings watched them approach. Their tails twitched with excitement. Leaving the safety of their bush, they gathered round Soar.

King Flylord clutched Soar in his paws. "My son, you have returned safely." Letting him go, Flylord studied him. "You are unhurt?"

"Yes father, I'm fine and so relieved to be here with you." Glancing at the other Kings, he smiled.

Speechless with joy, Flylord embraced him.

The others waited patiently, eager to hear about his adventure.

Trembling with excitement, Soar told them about his journey…the roaring monsters on the hard surface, and meeting the Oracle. "He is huge!" Soar told them, spreading his paws wide in emphasis.

"What does he look like?" King Pierro asked.

"He is like a huge rock with legs and a head," Soar said with a shiver. "His skin is scaly and he has long claws on his feet." Seeing their terrified expressions, he smiled. "He is frightening to look at, but he is also kind and wise." In a voice little more than a whisper, Soar said. "The Oracle has given me a new name."

"What is it? Tell us," his father and the other Kings urged.

"My new name is Soar. It means—"

"It means to rise, to fly upwards," Optimus said.

"Yes!" Soar exclaimed with excitement.

"And I'm sure you will," Optimus said. "With a great name comes great responsibility." Bowing his head he said. "I believe you have proved yourself before us all. There can be no doubt; you have shown yourself to be courageous, and selfless. However, now we must return to the others. For I know you have much wisdom to share with us."

As Optimus spoke, Soar's elation subsided. Remembering what the Oracle had told him to do, his shoulders drooped. The responsibility weighed heavy on him. *How will I remember everything he told me? How do I tell father, he must release the captives?* His chest felt uncomfortably tight, he could hardly breathe. Lowering his head, he sighed.

Knowing his thoughts, Optimus came alongside and gently encouraged him. "You are not alone," he said. "I will always be there to advise and help, if you need me."

Lifting his head, Soar raised a paw and brushed the moisture from his eyes. "Thank you," he said. Knowing he could rely on Optimus renewed his courage and strength.

The sun was high in the sky by the time the small party reached the den of King Ludus. Their arrival caused much excitement…everyone was elated to see them return safely. Surrounding Soar, they clamoured to hear about the Rat Run and his experience with the Oracle.

Soar struggled to suppress a yawn. He wanted to tell them, but was so exhausted, he could hardly think straight.

Seeing his tiredness, Optimus intervened, and told them all to get some rest. "We will meet later this evening," he said.

Sighing with relief, Soar curled up with his father. He felt safe again. Wrapping his long tail over his nose, he closed his eyes and went to sleep.

As evening approached, Optimus was the first to wake. Rousing the rest of the den, he summoned everyone to King Ludus's large chamber. The space couldn't accommodate them all, but it didn't matter, as Optimus and the Kings had already decided that for the first time in many years, every single rat, and all those involved in any way would meet at the Council Clearing in Grendeen Woods.

The Clearing was seldom used. It was a hallowed and sacred place. Whatever was decided there was law, and could not be changed.

The Clearing was available to any animals or birds, with a serious dispute, or a problem that needed sorting out. The last time a meeting was held there, Optimus had to preside over a situation between magpies and squirrels.

While everyone in the den shared a light breakfast, Optimus busied himself dispatching sparrows to the dens of King Pierro and King Flylord, requesting everyone's presence at the meeting.

At King Flylord's den, the arrival of the sparrow caused great excitement. Liza, and Seamist, could hardly contain themselves in their eagerness to know if their father and brother were safe and well.

They were shocked…yet proud, when they heard their brother, Prince Timere had drawn the short straw, compelling him to do the Rat Run. A feat they were relieved to hear, he had accomplished successfully. Hearing his new name, Prince Soar, they squealed with delight. Everyone in the den was thrilled by the news, and made hurried arrangements to leave for the meeting.

Prince Malar, Princess Shamrock and Crystal, eagerly joined in with the rest of the den's inhabitants preparing for the journey. Prince Malar's wounds had healed well. He was strong and quite his old self again.

No longer under guard, he'd spent a lot of time with Seamist. Their blossoming friendship annoyed Liza, but with her father King Flylord away, she grew bored of spying on them.

And so with the sparrow flying ahead, and Prince Malar taking the lead, the rats commenced the dangerous journey to the Council Clearing.

✥✥✥✥

At King Pierro's den, Seed the pigeon greeted the arrival of the sparrow. She took it upon herself to tell everyone the good news.

Princess Pecan danced around, beside herself with excitement…so relieved to hear Malar, Piper and her father were safe and that soon they would be reunited.

Aunty Freckle had quite a job keeping her calm, but with Rupert's help, she soon had Pecan and everyone in the den organised. Sky the rabbit and Seed were thrilled to be invited along.

Rupert looked forward to seeing Bluebear and Loki again. But the thought of journeying to the Council Clearing was a daunting prospect, one that made his heart race. All through the den, the other rats could feel the tension as they prepared for the journey.

Once they were ready to leave, the sparrow and Seed flew ahead, while the rats followed as fast as they could. Sky the rabbit, brought up the rear, his eyes and ears tuned for danger. However, the journey proved uneventful, as the inhabitants of Grendeen Woods, whether predator or prey, were aware a meeting of profound importance was taking place at the Council Clearing.

The moon was high in the sky by the time Seed led her party into the Clearing. There were gasps and loud oohs and ahs at the sight which greeted them!

Youngsters like Pecan and Rupert had never seen anything like it. They huddled together…eyes wide, their hearts racing.

Adding to the spectacle, the moon's soft glow, bathed everyone in a strange ethereal light. The effect was mystical…ghostly. Tall trees, like the pillars of a great cathedral soared into the night sky. A fine grey mist floated over the ground, swirling around the trees. To those gathered in the Clearing, it appeared as though the great trees floated; the atmosphere was electric. Filled with reverence and awe, everyone spoke in hushed tones.

Optimus the owl stood on a massive flat stone, which formed a natural platform. The three Kings and

Soar stood beside him. Raising his wings, he called the meeting to order. His strong voice echoed round the Clearing as he ordered everyone to join their respective clans.

With as little fuss as possible, the rats grouped together. They stood quietly; all eyes glued to Optimus, waiting for him to speak.

Rising to his full imposing height, Optimus addressed them, explaining the seriousness of the meeting. He began by telling them about Timere, how the young Prince had faced the challenge of the Rat Run, hoping to survive and meet the great Oracle.

"His bravery is most commendable," Optimus said. "The problems and strife between wild and fancy rats, has affected you all, for too long. But no one among you knew how to change the situation. That is until King Flylord's young son volunteered with two others, to do the Rat Run." Smiling, he glanced at Soar. "We are thrilled to tell you, he was successful in his quest to meet the Oracle, and has returned safely to us, much wiser for the experience."

The Clearing rang to loud cheers and clapping.

Raising a wing, Optimus called for order. "That's not all," he shouted above the excited murmurs. "The Oracle has blessed him with a new name. From now on, he will be known as Prince Soar."

Liza's tail swished with excitement. "He's my brother," she said proudly to anyone who would listen.

Overcome by it all, Pecan had to sit down. In the moonlight everyone looked like ghosts. *It's like a strange, but happy dream*, she thought.

Glancing at Soar, Optimus beckoned for him to come and address the waiting clans.

Soar expected to feel nervous…his heart raced, but with expectation, not fear. He felt surprisingly calm. Glancing up at Optimus, he saw the owl's large round eyes soften in an encouraging smile. "Go ahead young Prince, they will hear you."

"Are you sure?"

Optimus nodded.

Encouraged by the owl's confidence, Soar stepped to the edge of the rocky platform. For a moment the sight of so many expectant faces made him anxious. Closing his eyes, he took a few deep breaths and opened his mouth. The sound of his voice echoing around the Clearing took him by surprise.

Nevertheless, he soon got into his stride, as he told them about his journey across the hard surface, and his meeting with the Oracle. He explained about the ancient book of wisdom, and shared with them most of what the Oracle told him. Some he held back, knowing it was personal to him.

The Oracle's words were clear in Soar's mind, as though he were standing beside him. Soar's heart burned as they flew from his mouth. *I suppose I shouldn't be surprised*, he thought. *The Oracle told me I would remember everything.* Turning to his father, Soar said with an authority beyond his years. "The three captives must be returned to their fathers, at once."

Surprised by his son's demand, King Flylord's mouth dropped open. Nevertheless, he didn't argue. Motioning to Zadock, he ordered him to take the captives to their respective families.

King Ludus was thrilled to have his daughter, Princess Shamrock and her friend Crystal, safely returned to him. Tears trickled down his cheeks as he led them to where his small clan waited. Everyone was overjoyed to see them.

King Pierro hugged his son, Prince Malar. "It's good to have you back, my boy."

Old Bluebear was so pleased to see him; his grin nearly reached his ears.

Malar's brother and sister, Piper and Pecan jumped all over him, they were so excited.

Aunty Freckle, unable to contain her joy, put her paws round his neck and tried to groom him. "You've not looked after yourself," she said, giving him a gentle wash behind the ears.

∾∾∾

Prince Soar waited patiently for everyone to calm down. Once they were quiet and he had their undivided attention, he continued. He explained how important it was to communicate. Tearfully, he attempted to express his sorrow for the distress his clan had caused.

King Flylord nodded in agreement, his expression solemn…his eyes downcast.

When Soar finished speaking, to everyone's surprise, he left the platform and went first to King Pierro, and then to King Ludus. Taking their paws in his, he apologised for all that had taken place.

Both Kings were taken aback, but readily accepted him. They were relieved. At last things appeared to be improving. His overture of friendship…request for forgiveness slowly thawed the icy atmosphere of hatred and mistrust. Both Kings were impressed with the young Prince.

King Flylord followed his son's example and in no time he and Kings Ludus and Pierro were chatting openly.

Soar hurried across the clearing to speak with Prince Malar. His apology was accepted and as they talked Soar couldn't help noticing Malar's lovely sister, Princess Pecan.

Pecan's heart fluttered, her eyes widened as she returned his gaze.

Soar felt an excited shiver run up his spine. *She likes me*, he thought. He felt his heart would burst, so great was his sense of fulfilment and expectation. *This is how it should be, everyone happy…sharing resources, and helping each other*. Gazing round and listening to the animated chatter, he smiled. *It's so good to see everyone getting on. Life is too short for animosity and mistrust. Especially in a rat's case…our lives are short enough as it is*.

Optimus stood on the rock platform and flapped his wings. Raising his voice, he managed to make himself heard above the chatter. "Later, this coming night," he shouted. "There will be a feast at King Pierro's den, everyone is welcome." Rising to his full height he thanked them all for coming and declared the meeting over.

King Ludus, realising it would soon be dawn, invited King Flylord and his clan, to stay at his den and rest. "We could travel to the feast together." He suggested with a smile. "Safety in numbers, don't you think?"

King Flylord chuckled. "Indeed, it would be most acceptable, thank you."

Soar's heart fell, as he watched Pecan join her clan. Glancing at Seamist, he noticed her sad expression, and followed her gaze. Prince Malar was

85

leaving the Clearing with Pecan and the others. "You'll see him this evening," he said.

Seamist sighed. "I know, but I miss him already." Having noticed Soar's interest in Pecan, she said. "You like her, don't you."

Embarrassed, Soar lowered his head and admitted he did.

"But what about Princess Shamrock, I thought you liked her? She was captured for you."

"I know," Soar replied, wiping a paw over his long whiskers. "But I can't help the way I feel. From the moment I saw Princess Pecan, I could think of no one else."

Seamist smiled, "She is lovely and her brother Prince Malar is most handsome."

Soar noticed a fleeting sadness in her eyes. "What is it? What troubles you?"

"I just feel sad for Liza. I wish she could find someone," she said softly.

Soar was about to answer, when Liza ran up to them.

Breathless, she called. "Come on! Father says it's time to leave."

Following Liza they joined the rest of the clan; chatting happily as they journeyed to King Ludus's den.

The sound of bird song filled the air, an anthem to the rising dawn.

King Ludus and Flylord were aware of the danger and urged everyone to stay under cover as much as possible. So many rats traveling together were a tempting target. With Ludus taking the lead and Flylord bringing up the rear, they hurried everyone along, praying they would reach their destination safely.

Chapter Thirteen

King Pierro hurried through the woods, his mind occupied with the safety of his clan and the evening celebration. He could hear the youngsters chatting behind him. Glancing round, he called, "Stay close and keep your voices down." Hearing their excited giggles, he huffed and turned his attention to Seed flying ahead of him.

Prince Malar scampered to catch up with Pecan. Staring at her, he noted the faraway look in her eyes. "You like Prince Soar, don't you."

"Yes I do," she admitted. "I hope he likes me. Do you think father will mind?"

Malar smiled. "No, everything is different now; hopefully we are all going to be friends."

"I hope so," Pecan said. Glancing at him, she whispered. "The wild rats are not what I expected. They're like us really, but all the same colour."

"Except Seamist," Malar said. "She is different and so pretty. I really like her, she was kind to me."

They continued chatting as Piper caught up with them.

As they walked together, Malar asked him if he liked the Princess Shamrock.

Piper smiled. "She's lovely."

Malar nodded in agreement. "She was concerned about me," he told them. "She kept checking on me through Seamist. Without realising it, she brought us together." His voice dropped with emotion. "I will always be grateful to her."

"Isn't it wonderful?" Piper exclaimed. "We all have someone, and thanks to Prince Soar everything has turned out well.

Ahead, through the trees, they could see the den bathed in the light of early dawn. Everyone's pace increased.

Hopping ahead, Sky the rabbit kept an eye out for danger.

Seed the pigeon flew to a large tree close to the den. Resting on a branch, she mulled over all she'd seen and heard. Shaking her head, she murmured, "My, my, never did I imagine I would see such a day!" Smiling to herself, she tucked her head under her wing and dozed off. Her dreams filled with visions of the Clearing and Prince Soar's bold exhortation.

Optimus, having promised he would be at the feast in the evening, felt he needed a rest. "After all, I'm not getting any younger," he muttered as he glided on silent wings towards the oak tree he called home. Perched on a branch, he smiled. Things had turned out better than he could have hoped.

❧❧❧

Hurrying through the forest, Rupert and Bluebear stayed close to King Pierro. They noticed he seemed lost in thought.

"Is everything alright, Your Highness?" Bluebear asked. His eyes narrowed as he stared at the King.

Pierro glanced at him. "Yes, I'm merely thinking about the preparations for the feast this evening. I want it to be a time we will all remember. I see it as an opportunity to build bridges and cement new friendships."

Rupert and Bluebear, nodded in agreement. "It will be wonderful," Rupert said his dark eyes shining with excitement.

Bluebear's old face creased in a smile. "Indeed it will. The evening will be a great success."

Encouraged by their enthusiasm, and seeing the entrance to the den, King Pierro increased his stride.

Their arrival woke Seed. Cooing a greeting, she busied herself pecking the bark of the tree, in the hope of finding a quick snack.

Breathing heavily, King Pierro suggested everyone go and rest, as they would rise early to prepare for the feast.

No one argued, they were all tired after the excitement of the past few hours. Their heads buzzed with all they had seen and heard.

At first, fear had gripped them at the mention of the Rat Run, but then...overwhelming elation and relief, as their lives were turned around by one brave rat's sacrifice. Exhausted but happy, everyone went to their beds, aware there would never be such a time as this again.

Especially tired, and somewhat bemused by it all, old aunty Freckle disappeared to her bed ahead of them all.

Sky the rabbit, settled down with Rupert and Bluebear.

Malar, Pecan, and Piper were so excited, they didn't think they would sleep, but they curled up together and before anyone could count to ten, they were all gently snoring.

❧❧❧

Later that evening as the sun dropped below the horizon and a soft dusky light settled over the woods, the residents of the den slowly stirred.

Awake before everyone else, the youngsters were chatting with their father, King Pierro, in his chamber.

Pecan, keen to find out what he thought about Prince Soar, nestled against him, her bright eyes searching his face. "Do you like him father?"

Pierro chuckled. "If he likes you as much as you like him, then you have my blessing," he said.

Unable to contain herself, Pecan danced with delight.

King Pierro turned to Piper. "And you my son. Now you have seen her. How do you feel about Princess Shamrock?"

Piper smiled and closed his eyes. "I like her, father," he said softly.

"Then it seems to me, all my children are happy," King Pierro said with a merry twinkle in his eyes. "Now, off you go, we need to prepare for the feast. It won't be long before our guests arrive."

Bouncing out of his chamber; Prince Malar and Piper wrestled with each other, while Pecan jumped up and down squeaking with delight. Their noise woke the rest of the den and pretty soon everyone was mucking in, preparing for the feast.

King Pierro sat for a brief moment, enjoying the happy sounds. Grinding his teeth, his eyes bobbled with contentment. *It's been ages since I felt this relaxed*, he thought. *And it feels good.* He smiled, convinced from now on, all would be well.

Grooming his thick fur, his eyebrows rose as he reflected on the wild rats and the fact, he actually liked them. He was happy his son Prince Malar had fallen for King Flylord's young daughter Seamist. *I like her*, he thought. *And I must admit I'm surprised how well I get on with her father the King. It's amazing how much you have in common when you talk things through. It looks as though our two families will be united through our children.* His eyes sparkled with happiness at the thought.

Finishing his wash, King Pierro ambled round the den, keen to see how the preparations for the feast were coming along. Needless to say, Aunty Freckle had everything under control. Now all they could do was wait for evening and the arrival of the guests.

Chapter Fourteen

At King Ludus's den everyone was up and about. The air sparked with anticipation. The residents squeaked and chattered, as they scurried around making preparations to leave for the feast.

Kings Ludus and Flylord worked together organising the younger…excitable elements among them. Both Kings were amazed how well they got on. They had more in common than they realised.

King Ludus couldn't help a slight frown. He liked Prince Soar, which only heightened his disappointment that the young Prince seemed more interested in King Pierro's daughter Pecan, rather than his own daughter Shamrock. *Oh well*, he thought shrugging his heavy shoulders. *There's no time to worry about that now. We have a journey to make, and it's time to leave.*

The stars twinkled brightly in a cloudless sky, as they made their way out of the den and hurried to a small trail sheltered by thick shrubbery. All around, nocturnal life made its presence felt. Owls floated through the trees like grey ghosts on silent wings. A fox barked in the distance. The rats were alert…on tenterhooks, but determined not to let anything spoil their excitement.

Princess Shamrock, and Crystal, walked together chatting quietly.

Prince Soar walked up front, with his father and King Ludus.

While Zadock brought up the rear, ever on the lookout for trouble. His thick fur bristled at the thought.

Seamist followed her father and brother, preoccupied with thoughts of Prince Malar. Her tummy rolled with excitement at the thought of seeing him again.

Liza trotted along beside Zadock. She glanced at him, he seemed quieter than usual. Secretly Liza had always liked him. *I'm probably the only one who does*, she thought, wishing he would notice her. Liza sensed how her father felt about Zadock. She knew he respected him, but that was as far as it went. *If he knew how much I like Zadock, he wouldn't be so relaxed.* She thought with a wicked glint in her eye.

Walking side by side, Zadock and Liza were so alike; it was hard to tell them apart, except for Zadock's larger build.

"Are you alright?" Liza asked him.

Glancing at her, he raised a brow. "Yes, why do you ask?"

"No reason, you just seem quiet."

He looked at her intently for a moment, his one piggy eye searching her face.

Embarrassed, Liza dropped her gaze.

"I'm thinking, that's all." he replied.

"What are you thinking about?"

Moving closer to her, he whispered. "If you must know, I'm not happy about joining the fancy rats. It's wrong as far as I'm concerned. We've been around a lot longer than them. They've had human interference and I want no part of it." His tail twitched like an angry snake. His one eye flashed defiance. "I want to stay as I am, wild and free…answering to no one."

"You answer to my father!"

"Only because I want to; but now I'm not so sure. It looks to me like your father is going soft." Peering at her he grinned. "Anyway, I like having adventures, and fighting makes me feel alive."

Liza's heart fluttered at his closeness. Even with a missing eye, she found him irresistible. "I agree," she said. "When we captured Princess Shamrock, it was so exciting."

Zadock's eye widened as he looked at her. Tilting his head he asked. "Would you join me then? We could go away and start our own clan and show this motley crew what for."

Liza smiled, the idea appealed to her. She was wild and rebellious at heart; unlike her half-sister Seamist, and brother Prince Soar. "I will think about it," she said.

Zadock smirked; he could tell she was interested. He nudged her playfully with his shoulder.

Hearing her high pitched giggles, the others turned around.

Liza and Zadock grinned at each other, relishing the little secret between them.

King Flylord's brows met in an angry frown. *I wish she would walk with me. I don't want her getting involved with Zadock. But she's hard to control, always has been.* Glancing back he huffed. *Zadock's a bad influence!* Flylord knew he couldn't afford to give Zadock an inch…aware the young buck would contend for the leadership given half a chance. King Flylord hissed with anger. He knew Zadock was biding his time. One day he would make a move.

Flylord was still thinking about it as they entered a large meadow.

94

A soft breeze rustled the long grass; hiding under some bushes, they took a brief rest. A short way off, they saw large shadowy figures bobbing about.

"They're rabbits," Soar said with a relieved sigh.

A large rabbit left the group and hopped towards them. It was Sky's sister, Cloud.

King Ludus greeted her. "We're going to a feast, and your brother Sky will be there, come with us." Standing on his back legs, he called to the other rabbits. "Come, you're all welcome."

The rabbits were happy to join them. The little band crossed the meadow safely, and reached the woods on the other side. Under a canopy of trees and tall bracken, they felt a little safer. Slowly, they negotiated a path through the shrub roots and tall grass.

Hearing a soft swishing sound above them, and feeling a cool breeze ruffle their fur. They all knew it was an owl and immediately flattened their bodies to the ground.

Optimus chuckled as he descended silently in front of them. "It's only me," he said. "Sorry, I didn't mean to scare you."

Embarrassed, by their protective huddle, the rats quickly separated and hurried to greet him.

"Is everyone alright?" Optimus asked.

"Yes, we're all safe and relieved to see you," King Ludus said.

King Flylord smiled and nodded in agreement.

The others gathered round Optimus. His larger than life presence filled them with confidence.

After a brief moment of rest and refreshment, they followed Optimus. He flew low, gliding silently from branch to branch. The journey seemed never ending, but at last they crossed a piece of open ground and entered Windom Woods.

Merry sounds could be heard coming from King Pierro's den. Eagerly they increased their pace, not wanting to miss out on all the good food and fun.

Prince Malar saw them arrive and ran to greet Seamist. He was so thrilled to see her again, his heart raced.

Soar introduced himself properly to Pecan, who completely out of character, succumbed to unusual shyness.

Aunty Freckle smiled to herself, as she watched them sit together. Pecan suddenly coy…Soar for once tongue tied.

King Ludus took Shamrock to meet Piper. He couldn't help grinning at his son's nervous trembling and incoherent stammering.

Gazing adoringly at Shamrock, Piper took an inaudible breath. His mouth was so dry, he wasn't sure he could speak. In a choked voice, he said. "We thought we'd lost you." His legs trembled as he moved closer to her. Her silky fur gleamed like chocolate. The small white heart on her chest took his breath away. *She is beautiful!* Pulling himself together, he said softly. "It's wonderful to meet you at last."

Shamrock's eyes widened. Overawed by his presence her breath caught in her throat. "Thank you," she said softly.

"I will leave you both to get acquainted," King Ludus said. He was relieved to hear them talking as he lumbered off to get some food. He knew they needed time to get to know each other properly.

Sitting together, Zadock and Liza watched everyone.

Concerned, King Flylord raised his shoulders and strode over to them. "Come and join the party," he said, his eyes focused on Liza.

Looking away, she declined his invitation. "I'm happy here father, thank you."

Flylord tried to tempt her with food, but without success. He could sense Zadock's hostility to everything taking place, and felt sure he was planning something which involved his daughter. Struggling to remain calm, he gave Zadock, an 'I know what you are up to' look.

Normally Zadock would look away...bow his head. However, this time, he narrowed his eye and defiantly held the King's gaze.

His reaction was all Flylord needed to see. He knew something was up. Pumped with adrenalin and hot anger, the King fluffed his fur, making his body appear twice its size. His long thick tail swished and thrashed, hitting the ground with a thwacking sound. Turning his body sideways on, Flylord challenged Zadock, threatening him with attack.

He was an awesome sight, and Zadock backed off. No way did he want to tangle with him, not yet anyway. Zadock knew he wouldn't stand a chance. King Flylord was massive and powerful.

All of a sudden, Optimus appeared. Taking the situation in at a glance, he realised things were about to get nasty. Using all his diplomacy, he managed to distract King Flylord, before the situation got totally out of hand. "Come with me, Your Highness," Optimus said taking him over to the other Kings; who quickly noticed Flylord's agitated state.

"Is there something wrong?" King Pierro asked.

"Indeed there is," Flylord replied. "But I'm not sure what, at the moment." With his steely gaze fixed on Zadock, Flylord huffed with anger.

Optimus's large round eyes narrowed as he explained that Zadock could be out to cause trouble. With a deep sigh, he said. "Sadly, I believe young Liza has joined him." Something made Optimus turn his head as he spoke, the others followed his gaze…in time to see Zadock and Liza disappearing into the undergrowth.

King Flylord made to go after them, but Optimus and the other Kings stopped him.

"Let them go," Optimus said. "You won't change how they feel. There will be time to worry about them in the future. For now we will relax and enjoy this marvellous feast. They are in the minority. Our strength lies in being the majority and in doing the right thing."

His serious expression softened as he glanced round at them. "You have all joined forces under a banner of peace and unity, which is how it should be. Out of this unity will come strength and wisdom, enough to deal with the Zadock's of this world."

Unfurling a wing, he placed it round King Flylord. "As for Liza, she is young, but the time will come when she will see the truth for herself. Let her go…let her learn in her own way. It will be the making of her."

"I do hope you're right," Flylord said.

Hearing the sadness in his voice, Optimus, smiled reassuringly. "I know I am. Trust me, Liza will be back."

King Flylord sighed softly as they returned to the party, and settled down to enjoy the feast.

And what a spread it was, there was something for everyone to enjoy.

Sky the rabbit, had risked his life raiding a human garden to pick curly kale. A cabbage relished by the rats. The other treats on offer were wild berries, nuts, apples, fresh dandelion leaves and herbs, seeds, tasty grass, and nice cold water to drink.

They all had a wonderful time, and no one wanted the evening to end, especially the young ones lost in love.

The three Kings smiled as they watched the youngsters enjoying themselves. They were the new generation, destined to unite the three clans.

King Flylord's thoughts turned to Liza and sadness came over him, but it was fleeting. Watching his son Soar, and Pecan together, his heart swelled with pride. Entwining his small fingers, he embraced the hope rising within him.

Optimus flew onto the branch of a tree overlooking the den, and perched next to Seed.

As usual she had eaten too much, and could hardly move, let alone fly. Watching the scene below, her bright eyes shone with happiness. "I love romance," she cooed softly.

Optimus smiled to himself, he was happy to see everyone getting along so well; it was a tribute to Prince Soar's sacrifice and bravery…a justifiable reward for the risk he had taken. *So much has happened, in such a short time, but that's how it is with rats,* he thought. *They live their short lives in the fast lane.* Turning his large head nearly full circle, he muttered. "They are delightful creatures."

Seed looked up at him. "Yes, they are, and I'm glad Piper got his Princess after all." Watching the youngsters sit in a cosy little group, Seed sighed wistfully.

Optimus glanced at her, a good-humoured smile on his wise old face. He had to agree; seeing the young ones and their families united at last, was a rewarding sight. However, the disappearance of Liza and Zadock diminished his contentment somewhat. Optimus frowned, he knew Zadock could threaten everything the rats had achieved.

A cool breeze blew through the treetops ruffling his feathers. Hissing softly, Optimus huddled on his branch, he tried to rest, but try as he might, he couldn't shrug off a sense of foreboding….the ominous feeling that Liza's decision to follow Zadock, could threaten everything Prince Soar had achieved by doing the Rat Run.

Shaking his head, Optimus gazed into the woods. Below him, happy sounds from the party drifted on the night air. With a tired shrug, he closed his eyes. "All we can do is watch and wait," he said softly. "Watch and wait."

The Return

Part Two

Chapter One

The laughter and chatter coming from King Pierro's den, echoed through Windom Woods. The happy sounds followed Zadock and Liza, as they vanished among the trees.

Liza knew, following Zadock into the unknown, she was abandoning everyone she loved…leaving behind a life, that thanks to her brother Prince Soar, now seemed full of hope and promise.

Her brow furrowed as she allowed her mind to dwell on the past week. *It's amazing*, she thought, *like a dream*. She found it hard to believe, her young brother had succeeded in doing the Rat Run. Not only that, he'd survived the experience and now had a different name.

The memory of him standing on the stone platform in the Council clearing, the authority in his voice as he ordered the captives returned to their families, sent a tingle down Liza's spine. She couldn't deny the warmth she'd felt inside as she watched new friendships forged… forgiveness given and received. All of which culminated in the party, she and Zadock were leaving behind.

Running alongside Zadock, Liza questioned why she was leaving. *Could it be because my brother and sister and all the others, have found someone special?* Liza's eyes narrowed as she thought about it. She had to admit, she did feel left out; but was that the reason; she couldn't be sure. One thing she did know, she really liked Zadock.

If he'd chosen to stay, she would have been happy, but the new way of life was not for him. He wanted to go, and she had to go with him. Liza knew if she stayed with her family and let him go without her, she would have regretted it…wondered what exciting adventures she was missing out on. She had no doubts they were meant to be together, they were so alike. She felt alive when she was with him, but at what cost? Only time would tell.

Travelling deeper into Windom Woods, the darkness soon swallowed them. They could no longer hear the merriment coming from the den. High in a tree, an owl hooted.

Liza kept close to Zadock. She knew it wasn't Optimus, she'd seen him watching them as they'd slipped away. Breathless with running, her voice shook as she asked Zadock. "Where are we going?"

"As far away as possible," he replied. "We'll make a new life and a new clan together…keep the old ways alive."

The determined tone in his voice gave Liza confidence.

Using shrubs and long grass for protection, they managed to maintain a steady pace while avoiding danger; not least the owl.

Liza's lungs burned, her legs ached, but she pushed on.

Seeing her tiredness, Zadock stopped by a small stream. "We can shelter under this boulder." He said, gesturing with a paw. "There's plenty to eat, and we can drink from the stream." He glanced up at the sky. "Dawn is only a few hours away. We'll stay here and rest for a while."

With her tummy full, Liza relaxed as they curled up together. In no time they were fast asleep. When they woke it was early morning. A watery sun struggled to break through the dark clouds scudding across the sky.

"I hope it won't be stormy," Liza said, peering anxiously at the sky.

"It doesn't matter if it is, don't worry about it. We'll eat and then get going," Zadock insisted.

After a breakfast of tasty dandelion leaves, and a drink from the stream, they continued their journey. Leaving the protection of the woods they crossed some fields, and made their way slowly through a small clump of trees. It was mid-morning, and they were both in need of rest. They stopped by an old tree, which had a small hole near its base.

"This will do, it will make a good home for us," Zadock said.

Liza stared at the tree, not at all sure she agreed with him.

Zadock noticed her hesitation. "It will be fine, the ground is soft, and we'll be safe here. Trust me. If we dig down under the roots, we can make a nest, come on!" Using his front paws, he dug away at the soft soil, as if to encourage her.

Liza joined him, and in no time they excavated a deep hole under the tree. The entrance was small, hardly noticeable, but inside it was spacious. They lined the nest with dried moss and grass.

Liza inspected her new home and sighed with contentment. Zadock was right, they would be happy here. They'd survived the journey, and a strong bond was growing between them. She had chosen Zadock, and not for one moment did she regret it, or her decision to leave all she knew and follow him.

A few months later Liza became the proud mother of eight kittens. She and Zadock spent most of their time hunting for food. With so many mouths to feed, she had to keep her strength up. Sadly, a couple of days later she lost three of her babies, but that only made her more determined to raise the remaining five. Zadock was a good father, and did his best to help her.

The kittens were coming up to three weeks old, full of energy, and always hungry.

Nevertheless, even with the demands of motherhood, Liza was happy, she and Zadock made a good team. Life had its dangers, but with Zadock beside her, she felt she could overcome anything. He was strong and brave, and seemed to fear nothing. Even with his one eye, he was a match for any other rat. And so far they had managed to avoid any large predators. She was beginning to think they were invincible!

Zadock often left the nest to wander alone, but always returned around dawn with a treat for Liza. It was during one of his nocturnal ramblings, that he came across a small farm. On closer inspection he noticed the farmer reared a lot of chickens.

He raced back to Liza, his heart pounding with excitement. The words tumbled over each other, as he tried to tell her about the tasty grain and large fresh eggs. "There might even be a small chicken we can kill and bring back for our young ones to try," he said eagerly.

Liza couldn't help smiling at the sparkle she saw in his eye. Nevertheless, concern tempered her own enthusiasm. She knew there would be other rats there, who would defend their territory, and who knows what other dangers. Not only that, it was further than she wanted to go. It would mean leaving her babies for longer than usual.

Zadock could see the doubt in her eyes, but he insisted, assuring her the babies would be fine. Eventually, he managed to persuade her, and it was decided they would go later that night.

Liza spent an uneasy day resting, and nursing her young ones. "Your father and I will be away for longer tonight," she told them. "You must remain in the nest and be as quiet as possible." Closing her eyes, she sighed. *I hope they understand, their lives depend on it.* Raising her head, she glanced at her squirming, squeaking babies…her heart fluttered with love and concern.

When evening approached, and the time came to leave, Liza was not at all happy. The darkness of the night was her only comfort…storm clouds covered the moon, thunder rumbled in the distance. Liza trembled; this was one adventure she was not happy about.

Zadock bristled with determination and excitement as he led her into the darkness.

Chapter Two

Liza hurried after Zadock, every nerve taut with anxiety. She took an inaudible breath when they reached the farm, and sheltered under a low bush. A short distance away there stood a large farmhouse...its bright lights breaking the darkness. Trembling with excitement, she huddled close to Zadock. Now they were there, she had only one thought on her mind... get to the chicken run. Impatient to get moving and return to her babies, Liza crawled forward, leaving the protective cover of the bush.

"Wait"! Zadock hissed. "I can smell a dog."

Crouched under the bush, they waited. Zadock's nose twitched as he sniffed the air, cautiously he crept forward. "It seems okay, follow me," he whispered. The chicken run was just ahead of them, they could hear the birds inside clucking.

Moving as one, they crawled through a gap in the wire, and found a small hole into the hut. Their eyes soon adjusted to the darkness. Seeing all the birds sitting on perches; both rats trembled with excitement.

The chickens squawked and flapped their wings. Dust and feathers floated in the air.

Zadock struggled to make his voice heard above the noise. "Look, here are some eggs," he shouted.

Liza left the seed scattered on the floor and followed him.

The chicken, sitting on the eggs, watched them approach. Squawking hysterically, she pecked and flapped at Zadock, but her attempts to protect her eggs was useless.

Zadock's angry hissing drove her from the nest. She flew to a high perch, and joined the other hens, who were protesting loudly at the intrusion and theft.

The rats smashed a couple of eggs, and were enjoying the contents. However, their pleasure was short lived, as footsteps could be heard running towards the henhouse. Realizing they were in danger, they squeezed through the hole, leaving the tasty eggs behind; their hunger superseded by their desperate need to escape.

Scrambling back under the wire, they found themselves face to face with an angry terrier. The small dog stood his ground, his fur bristling, his lips curled back revealing sharp white teeth. He yapped with frenzied excitement for the farmer and made a lunge for Zadock, catching him by the back leg.

The big rat twisted round, and bit the dog on the cheek. It yelped and let him go.

Zadock made a run for it, but his injured leg let him down, and the dog managed to force him into a corner.

Liza crouched under a bale of hay, her fur fluffed, eyes wide with fear, as she watched Zadock fight for his life.

Scowling, the farmer arrived on the scene, his gun loaded and ready. However, when he saw it was rats, and not a fox, he stood back and yelled encouragement to the dog.

The plucky terrier made another grab for Zadock, and this time he got him by the back of the neck. Struggling for his life, Zadock's loud squeals were drowned by the dog's angry growls and the farmer's delighted shouts.

Making brief eye contact with Liza, and with his last breath Zadock cried, "Go, quickly."

Keeping out of sight, Liza ran out from under the bale of hay. Stopping briefly, she looked back. The dog was shaking Zadock as though he were a rag doll. She could see he was dead.

⋘⋘⋘

Frozen with grief, for a moment she stood there, before swinging round and fleeing into the woods…Zadock's command to go, ringing in her ears. Her lungs burned, her breath floated on the cold air. Every muscle ached, but she pushed on, running as fast as she could back to the nest and her kittens. They were hungry and pleased to see her.

Trembling with fear, and the shock of what she'd seen, she lay down and nursed them. Gazing at their tiny bodies writhing and squirming, her heart ached. "How will I manage alone?" she said softly.

The next few days were hard for Liza. Without Zadock's help, she was forced to forage more frequently to keep her strength up, but afraid to go far from the nest because of predators, her diet was limited. With a shortage of nourishing food and suckling her babies, Liza's strength and condition deteriorated. In the daylight hours as they huddled in the nest, her thoughts would turn to her father, King Flylord, and the family back in Tamwood forest. She wondered if they missed her…wondered if her father was alright? Homesickness tugged at her heart.

However, once the babies started to eat solid food, things improved a little. Liza's strength returned and she had more energy, which was just as well, as her kittens were bundles of energy, and full of questions. Understandably, they all wanted to know where their father was. As gently as she could, Liza tried to explain what had happened.

There were tears of sadness, but one little buck, so like his father, stomped around the nest on shaky legs…baby fur all fluffed up, as he told them what he would do to that farm dog, when he was grown up. He looked so amusing, it made them laugh, cloaking the sad atmosphere for a second or two.

For a few more days they stayed in the nest. Liza was loath to leave, as this was the home Zadock had found for her. Nevertheless, she had come to a decision. She knew she must return to her father, king Flylord.

Her kittens were strong and Liza felt confident they could make the journey. She knew they must leave, alone they would not survive. A tear trickled down Liza's face as she thought of the little doe she lost the night before…snatched by an owl. Now, she only had four kittens, and predators were becoming aware of their presence.

With a heavy heart, she made the decision to leave and go home. *Better to die trying to get home, than stay here and be picked off,* she thought. She trembled as another thought entered her head. *What if my father won't take me back? I wouldn't blame him, but I have to try, it's our only hope.* Liza knew, without Zadock they would never survive.

Gathering her remaining kittens together, she told them the whole story from beginning to end, and tried to prepare them for the long and dangerous journey back to their grandfather's den…back to a way of life she and Zadock had rejected, but a way of life she must again embrace. Like a prodigal she must return, and throw herself on her father's mercy.

Liza had to admit, she missed her father and her family. But another part of her had enjoyed the excitement of being with Zadock. He'd always been so wild and free, but now he was gone.

A very different Liza would return to her father. She had learned a lot, and was much wiser and certainly more mature. To be alone was not natural for a rat. She knew if they were to survive, they needed to be with their own kind. Not just for company, but for safety.

The decision made, Liza could hardly wait to get going. Suddenly she was desperate to see her family again. However, she had to be patient for a few more days; by then her kittens would be more able to cope. Each day made a difference to their growth and strength, as she prepared them for the long journey that lay ahead.

Chapter Three

A thick blanket of clouds concealed the moon. Liza's eyes brightened, she knew the darkness would work in their favour. *Not a bad night to start our journey,* she thought.

She had decided earlier in the day, that this would be the night to leave. She felt sure her kittens were strong enough to cope. She could not afford to wait much longer. Liza decided, they would travel by night, and rest during the day. Hopefully, with it being so dark, predators won't notice us. Her body tensed, she knew she was deceiving herself. The thought of her young ones in danger and frightened made her heart thump in her chest. *I hope the journey won't take too long.* Having made the decision to return home, her only desire now, was to see her father King Flylord and re-join her clan. "If they'll have me," she said softly.

Earlier in the day, she'd called the family together, and did her best to prepare them for the journey. The den echoed to the youngster's animated chatter, as they tucked into a meal of nuts, seeds, and dandelion leaves. Their eyes bright with excitement, they tried to heed their mother's words of warning.

Liza did her best to make them understand the dangers they could encounter. Nevertheless, their innocent enthusiasm amused her.

Her sons, Corsi and Solo, in many ways resembled their father. Corsi, especially, was a real chip off the old block. Impulsive and a little quick tempered, but full of courage, like his father.

Her two daughters were smaller, but fit and healthy; especially Almond. Liza would often smile as she saw herself in her daughter…that same tenacity and insatiable curiosity.

Hazel, the youngest by a few minutes was quiet and sensitive. She was the smallest, and seemed rather nervous. From the moment Hazel was born, Liza saw the likeness to her brother Soar, and couldn't help giving her a little extra love. She hoped in time, Hazel would truly resemble her uncle Soar, and grow in size and courage. *Nevertheless, Zadock their father would be proud of them all,* she thought.

Thinking of Zadock brought a stab of pain to Liza's heart. She missed him, especially now. He was always so strong and confident. *How will I manage without him?*

Tears moistened her dark eyes, as she recalled the fateful night at the farm. In her mind's eye, she could still see the terrier shaking him like a rag doll. The terrifying image was indelibly printed on her mind. She hoped in time, it would fade from her memory.

Almond's voice broke in on her thoughts. "Mother when are we leaving?"

Hearing the impatience in her daughter's voice, Liza smiled. "Soon, but first eat your food; it could be the last we get for a while."

Little Hazel sighed and snuggled up to her mother. "I will miss our home. I wish we didn't have to leave." Her small pink ears drooped, as she took a last wistful look around the cosy little nest.

The next minute, she squealed in protest, as Almond and the two boys piled on top of her in rough play. "Don't be such a baby! We're going on an adventure." Their voices rose with excitement.

Liza stood and called them to order. "Enough, be quiet! We are leaving now. Remember what I told you. Stick close together, and keep your eyes on me at all times. When I tell you to do something, do it! Especially you Corsi, do you hear me"?

"Yes, mother," Corsi said, peering at her under his lashes.

Hiding her smile, Liza gazed at them. "Are you ready to go?" She asked.

The youngsters responded with loud squeaks of excitement.

෧෧෧

Liza's heart raced as she led them into the dark night. The wind whistled through the tree tops. Long branches rustled and swayed above their heads.

The youngsters stayed close behind their mother.

"What's that noise? I don't like it," Solo whispered.

Liza smiled and told him it was just the wind.

Corsi trotted beside her. "What's wind?" He asked.

Struggling to remain patient, Liza did her best to explain, while at the same time keeping them moving as fast as she could.

A few hours had past, and they hadn't got very far. She knew her father's den was to the west, and their journey would take them close to the woods, where Optimus the owl lived. Liza knew the journey would be long, and was beginning to wonder if they should have stayed put. No! She thought, and increased her pace.

114

We must keep going, we will make it…we have to. If we can get to where Optimus lives, we stand a chance.

The thought of old Optimus the owl, filled her with renewed confidence. Once they reached his woods, she might be able to relax a bit. She knew he would be more than willing to help them. Frowning, she glanced round at the youngsters. "We'll need all the help we can get," she muttered.

Moving in single file, the youngsters were learning to be alert, and becoming aware of their surroundings.

Perched on a high branch above their heads, an owl hooted. The eerie sound had them scurrying to safety.

"Down, keep low," Liza hissed. They moved fast following their mother, as she scrambled under a rotten log.

"We will be safe here for a while, you need a little rest anyway."

"Can I sleep now, mother?" Hazel asked. "I'm really tired."

Liza looked with concern at her young daughter. "Yes you can, just for a while," she said softly.

The two boys had found a grub in the rotten bark, and a heated argument arose as to who should have it.

"I found it," Solo complained.

Corsi snatched it from his brother, and turned his back.

Solo huffed, but he wasn't too bothered, the old log was home to plenty more, enough for them all.

Snuggled under the log…tummies full of tasty grubs, the little family rested. Liza knew they would need all their strength to continue their journey.

Chapter Four

A few miles away, outside a small village, a group of gypsies were camped in a farmer's field. Their gaily painted caravans, horses and livestock, gave the small field a carnival air. The gypsies had been there about a week, finding whatever work they could in the surrounding farms and villages.

Chester, an old sheep dog, lay under his master's caravan, trying to keep cool. Even though there was a breeze, it was still a warm night. His long pink tongue lolled out of his mouth as he panted.

He had been with his master ever since he was a puppy. But now he was old and tired. Usually his master would trim his long coat when it got hot, but he hadn't done it as yet. Chester hoped he would soon, as it was becoming matted and uncomfortable. The old dog sighed and rested his chin on his paws. He enjoyed his life with the gypsies. His master was a hard man, but not cruel.

Travelling constantly from place to place was not easy for any of them. They made their living collecting scrap, or doing whatever work came their way. His master also kept a small flock of goats, which Chester enjoyed rounding up. However, his favourite job was going hunting with his master and the other men. Lately though, he seemed to have very little energy, and now his master was more interested in the new pup he'd bought at a local fair. Chester would listen to his master extolling its virtues, as he sat round the camp fire in the evening with the other men.

The old dog sighed as he remembered the good old days. *It's the way he used to talk about me,* he thought.

His ears pricked as his mistress came down the caravan steps and threw a small bone to him.

"Don't waste good food on the old dog," the master shouted at her. "If they don't work, they don't eat…simple as that. It's the pup what needs feeding up," he grumbled.

"Well I've got a bone for him too," she replied impatiently. "You shouldn't turn your back on old Chester; he's been a good dog."

"I know that woman, but times is hard, and you know our rules as well as me. There's no free ride for any of us. If you don't work you don't eat, and you know what I gotta do, and it ain't easy, so don't keep going on at me. I'll take him into the woods tomorrow."

"There's no harm in the old boy having one last bone, if his teeth can chew on it," she snapped. Muttering to herself, she returned to the caravan.

Chester lay under the van, enjoying his bone; he wondered why his master was taking him into the woods tomorrow. *Maybe, we are going rabbiting. Maybe, he wants me to train that whipper-snapper of a pup.* His tail wagged at the thought.

The next day dawned bright and sunny. Chester came out from under the caravan and had a good long stretch.

The pup ran to greet him, but reaching the limit of his chain, was brought up short. Annoyed, he started to yap, jumping up and down with frustration.

"Quiet down or you'll be in trouble," Chester warned.

It was early and most people in the camp were still asleep.

An old horse swished her tail with annoyance. "Stop your noise pup; you'll get us all in trouble."

"I want to play," the puppy whined.

"Well, it's too early," Chester growled.

Twirling around and grumbling with annoyance, the pup settled down in the grass.

The fire in the middle of the camp still glowed; the coals were hot and smouldering. The women would soon bring it back to life, when they prepared their menfolk's breakfast over it. Then the camp would be alive with noise and activity, and best of all, the intoxicating smell of frying bacon. Chester drooled at the thought.

He'd loved the gypsy life…loved roaming the countryside, and seeing different places. But now he felt old and tired, and just wanted a quiet life. His old bones ached in the winter, and in the summer the heat sapped his strength. These days, he struggled with the constant upheaval and travelling.

But it was in his blood, this gypsy life. He could never settle for any other way. What was an old gypsy dog to do? What was his future to be? He had no illusions about his master, he was a hard man; they all were. Life made them that way.

Sighing deeply, Chester curled up under the caravan, enjoying the coolness of early dawn. He tried not to think of the future. Closing his eyes he dozed off, getting lost in his dreams; so many rabbits to chase, and goats to herd and watch over.

Chapter Five

Liza and her kittens had spent the day resting deep inside a hollow tree, they had put a few miles between themselves and the old nest. *But it's not enough,* Liza thought, her tail twitched with agitation. The youngsters, even Corsi, were beginning to struggle, and she began to wonder if they would make it. Little Hazel was finding the journey particularly difficult, but she put a brave face on it. Even so, it was obvious to Liza; her young daughter was not coping at all well.

She sighed as she watched her young ones sleeping, curled up together, so sweet and innocent. Protective love filled her aching heart. Gently she washed the small body nearest to her.

Solo moaned, roused by the gentle touch of her tongue. Raising his head, he asked. "What mother?"

Liza smiled. "Nothing, rest awhile longer, and then we must make a move."

He needed no second bidding; snuggling down with his siblings he fell asleep, warm and safe.

As the sun slowly dipped beyond the horizon, Liza left them resting, and cautiously went out to find food. "They will need their strength," she murmured. Rooting around the base of the tree, she found some tasty nuts and dandelion leaves. Filling her mouth as full as she could, she carried the food to the nest. After a few trips, she had enough and woke them. They were all hungry and feasted well. After eating, they had a quick wash and left the relative safety of the hollow tree.

The path they followed took them through open fields, with many dangers to look out for. The moon was high in the sky, making them an easy target for birds of prey.

Liza sighed with relief when they pushed through a deep hedge, and came out into a field of long grass. Now they had some cover, and she felt safer.

Some field mice were playing; chasing each other around. When they saw the rat family, they ran back to their nest squeaking. "You had best watch out," they cried. "There's a fox in this area."

"Thank you," Liza replied. "We will keep our eyes open."

Moving on, they kept as close together as they could. The youngsters were more confident, and wanted to play.

Liza trembled with anxiety. Even concealed in the long grass, this was a dangerous place. She wouldn't feel safe until they were back in the woods. The long grass swayed gently in the breeze. Liza stopped, her long whiskers twitched as she sniffed the air.

Corsi, started playing with a long piece of grass. Much to his annoyance, his sister Almond, got hold of the other end. They were about to argue, when Liza ordered them to be quiet and lie down.

"Why mother?" Solo asked.

"Just do it," she hissed.

Hearing the urgency in her voice, the youngsters huddled together in the grass.

Liza couldn't be certain, but above the sound of the swaying grass, she could hear something else moving. Crouching low, she strained to hear, and then to her horror, she smelt it…the strong acrid smell of fox.

The youngsters smelt it too. They had no idea what a fox was, nevertheless they knew they were in danger, but there was nowhere to hide. They could only hope, concealed in the tall grass, the fox wouldn't catch their scent.

All of a sudden, the grass was roughly pushed aside, as a large rabbit shot past them, its ears flat back…eyes wide with terror. A large fox followed close behind. Neither the fox, nor the rabbit noticed the rats. The rabbit raced flat out, twisting and turning through the grass…desperate to shake off its pursuer, but the fox was young, fast and hungry.

The rabbit made a quick turn, but lost its footing, and fell. It struggled to regain its feet, but too late, the fox was on it in a second. The end came swiftly. All the rats heard was the rabbit's high pitched cry…then silence, except for the breeze rustling through the grass.

"What happened mother?" The youngsters asked.

Hearing the fear in their voices, Liza explained as gently as she could. "I'm afraid the fox killed the rabbit."

Little Hazel started to cry, and nestled up close to her mother. The others did the same.

Liza did her best to comfort and reassure them, and after a while they calmed down, and were able to resume their journey. The long grass thinned out, as they made their way across a field. Ahead of them, they saw holes in the ground, and large grey shapes bobbing about.

"What are they?" Solo asked.

"They're rabbits," Liza replied.

Catching site of the rats, the rabbits bunched together. "Who are you? What do you want?"

It was obvious to Liza; the fox's presence had made them nervous. She did her best to explain. "We are returning to my father in Tamwood," she said.

"Did you see the fox chasing the rabbit; did it get away?" One of the rabbits asked, in a shaky voice.

Liza swallowed and lowered her head. She knew she must tell them what she'd seen and heard. "As far as I know, the fox killed the rabbit," she said softly. "We heard a cry and a scuffle. I'm really sorry. I do hope I am wrong."

A big buck rabbit stepped forward and broke the awkward silence. "I doubt you're wrong," he said. "This happens a lot to us. Most nights the fox or an owl takes one of us. However, it's not something you ever get used to."

He looked closely at Liza and her little ones. "You all look tired," he said. "Why not rest awhile with us; you will be safe in our burrows. It will soon be dawn and your young ones look spent."

Liza had to agree, they were tired. Gratefully she accepted his kind offer.

The big rabbit introduced them to the others in his group, before leading them to his burrow. He brought them some food, and showed them where they could sleep. "You'll be safe and comfortable here," he said.

"You are kind, thank you," Liza said taking a large dandelion leaf in her paws. She hadn't realized how hungry she was.

Corsi and Solo forgot about food, in their desire to explore the burrow.

However, Liza would have none of it. "Remember your manners; this is not your home. We are guests," she said sternly.

"Sorry mother," the two boys said, staring shame-faced at the ground.

Liza attempted to conceal a smile as she urged them to eat something. "When you've finished your food, go to bed. We must rest; we have a long journey tomorrow."

Hazel and Almond, worn out after the excitement and trauma of the last few hours, were already asleep, curled up together on the soft mossy bed.

For a while, Liza and the rabbit, who introduced himself as Parsley, sat together quietly chatting.

"Why are you going on such a long and dangerous journey?" He asked.

"We need to get back to my father and the rest of my family."

There was silence for a moment, as the rabbit sat deep in thought. "Does your father have a son called Soar?"

"Soar is my brother," Liza exclaimed with excitement. "How do you know him?"

Parsley smiled at her. "Everyone knows Soar, he is a wise and gentle Prince, and has brought peace and unity to his kingdom. Your father the King is old now. I hope you get home in time. Tamwood is quite a way from here."

Liza could see the concern in his eyes. "We will make it," she said, a determined tone to her voice.

They chatted for a while longer. It turned out Parsley was related to Sky, and Cloud, the two rabbits, which had looked after Rupert and the other rats, after the battle to kidnap Princess Shamrock.

Liza felt awkward and didn't really want to talk about that episode. She felt ashamed that she had played a part in it. Her great desire now was to get home to her father, and hopefully, find forgiveness and acceptance.

Yawning with tiredness, she thanked Parsley for his hospitality, and joined her sleeping kittens to rest, they still had a long way to go, and would need all their strength.

Chapter Six

In the gypsy camp, Chester scrambled to his feet, yawned, and shook the dust from his coat. Wagging his tail, he greeted the mistress as she came down the caravan steps.

"Morning boy," the mistress said as she walked over to the fire. Grabbing a length of wood, she prodded the grey embers back into life, and threw on some fresh logs. The fire was soon blazing away, ready for the women to cook breakfast for their men-folk.

In no time, the camp was a buzz of noise and activity. Thick strips of bacon sizzled in a large black pan…strong coffee in a big communal pot, brewed by the side of the fire.

Chester loved this time of day; the smell of bacon made his mouth water. He lived in hope he might get some. Occasionally, he and some of the other dogs were thrown bits of bacon rind.

The pup, jumped about, yapping his head off; the children made things worse by teasing him.

"Leave him be!" Chester's master shouted from the caravan.

The kids scattered, and a semblance of order came over the camp. One of the women threw Chester and the pup a crust of bread each. She'd wiped it around the bacon pan, it was delicious.

Chester lay under the van, licking the tasty bacon grease off his whiskers.

The gypsies sat around finishing their breakfast and chatting. Some were already harnessing the horses, ready to go into the towns and villages, to collect scrap.

After an hour or so, the master came for Chester; he was carrying a thick rope. "Come on boy," he muttered, tying the rope round the old dog's neck.

Chester wagged his tail, he was glad to be going out again with his master, but couldn't understand why he had to wear a rope. He was used to being free, but he didn't mind; his master was carrying a gun and that meant they were going hunting. Then to his horror, the master unchained the pup and put a lead on him.

"Oh no," Chester moaned. "He's not coming as well."

"Yes I am," the pup yapped, leaping about with excitement.

"Settle down," the master growled, yanking hard on the lead. The pup yelped and cringed at his feet.

Chester could see the mistress watching them. He couldn't understand why she looked so sad.

The master led them out of the camp, and headed for the woods. It was a good mile up hill, and Chester found it hard work. He could feel his heart thudding in his chest. He looked forward to reaching the shade of the trees, and relished the chance to show the pup how to catch a rabbit or two.

At last, they left the open road and were soon under a canopy of leaves. The air was cool...silence enveloped them. All they could hear was the sound of their footsteps crunching on dry twigs and leaves, and the occasional bird protesting at the intrusion.

Chester loved this place; over the years he'd spent many happy hours roaming and hunting in these woods. They walked for another hour or so, and

Chester began to wonder where they were going; this area was new to him.

The master led them a bit further before stopping by a tall tree. He tied the pup to a low bush, and led Chester to the tree. Roughly, he pulled the old dog close into its trunk.

Chester could feel the rough bark against the side of his face. His furry brow wrinkled as he watched his master walk round and round the tree, until there was no rope left. It was wound tightly around the trunk of the tree…so tight Chester couldn't move his head. He felt he would choke, and started to struggle and cry.

"Well this is it, old boy, I'm sorry it has to be this way."

Chester watched him stoop and pick up his rifle from the ground. It was then the realization dawned. Whimpering, he gazed into his master's face, his soft brown eyes pleading with him. With strangled cries, he struggled against the rope, choking and growling.

The master raised the gun and strode towards him. "Stay still now, good dog."

Suddenly, a rabbit shot out of a nearby bush, and streaked past them.

The pup went crazy! Struggling and yapping, he slipped his collar, and flew off in pursuit of the rabbit, barking his head off and howling.

Furious, the master cursed and yelled at the top of his voice, but to no avail. There was nothing for it. He would have to leave Chester, until he got the pup back. So with his gun under his arm, he ran after the pup, following the sound of its excited barking.

The rope around Chester's neck grew tighter, saliva dripped from his mouth as he struggled to swallow. His body shook with fear as he realized he couldn't get free, and his master intended to kill him. Panting, he tried to stay calm. He knew somehow he must escape, but how? He was sure his master would be back.

He stood there, for what seemed like hours. He guessed it must be late afternoon as it was beginning to get dark. Tiredness sapped his strength, his legs shook, and every muscle ached. He tried to chew on the rope, but it was wound so tightly around the tree that his old teeth just couldn't bite through it. The only result from his efforts was blood on the rope and sore gums.

His heart sank when it dawned on him…the master had left him there to die. Raising his head, he tried to howl, but the sound was a strangled whimper. No one could hear, and no one came. He was alone, and it was dark. All around, the trees looked like ghostly sentinels, content to watch him dying. High on a branch an owl hooted. The eerie sound heightened Chester's fear.

All of a sudden, a soft rustling caught his attention, his ears pricked. He struggled to see, but the rope was too tight. His heart pounded. *Is my master coming back?* His eyes widened with fear. He listened intently, but as the sound came closer, he realized the footfall was too soft for human feet, and relaxed a little. However, when he saw what it was, his heart sank.

Chapter Seven

Liza and her youngsters were curled up fast asleep, when Parsley the rabbit came in with some food; he gently woke them. "It's past dawn, and you said you wanted to make an early start."

"Thank you," Liza said. She woke the youngsters and gave them some food.

Parsley sat and watched them. "Did you sleep well?"

With her mouth full of leaves, Liza nodded.

Parsley smiled. "It's going to be a hot day; the sun's already high in the sky." Inclining his head, he asked. "Should you be traveling in daylight?"

Liza shook her head. "What difference does it make? Last night, sadly, one of your own died. Maybe in daylight there will be fewer predators around. Either way I have no choice, we must make the journey."

After finishing their breakfast, they followed him out of the burrow into the morning sunshine. Liza felt her spirit lift. "Thank you for your hospitality," she said to Parsley. "You have been most kind."

Parsley smiled. "You're welcome. I wish you a safe journey home." Raising a paw, he pointed at the distant woods. "That's the way you need to go, once in the woods you should be safer."

Liza thanked him, and hurried her small family into the long grass. The woods looked a long way off; she hoped they would make it safely.

The youngsters were full of energy, running and playing behind her. "Don't make too much noise," she rebuked gently. "We are never far from danger."

But they were too busy enjoying themselves to heed her warning.

They were more than half way across the meadow. Ahead, the woods beckoned to them, offering shelter and protection.

Suddenly, the ground beneath their feet trembled. The morning stillness shattered by a sound like thunder. Shaking with fear, the rats huddled together as the thunder came closer.

"What is it mother?" the youngsters shouted, trying to make themselves heard above the terrifying noise.

Liza had no idea, but she knew they were in grave danger. Her fear was confirmed, when the grass near them parted, and their rabbit friends shot past, followed by some terrified field mice. "Run, quick!" The mice squeaked. "It's the farmer, he's cutting the meadow, and he's coming this way."

Liza and her family needed no second bidding. Joining the others they ran as fast as they could towards the safety of the woods. Cowering in a hedge they looked back. Through a thick cloud of dust, they could see the top of a huge metal monster. It appeared to eat the grass and spew it out behind, leaving in its wake a field full of small bales.

"Mother where is Hazel?" Corsi cried above the noise. Liza felt as if her stomach dropped to the ground. Wide eyed with panic, she stared around. "We must find her," she cried.

Desperate with worry, they all shouted and shouted for her, but no response. In blind panic, Liza ordered the remaining youngsters to stay where they were. Taking a deep breath, she prepared to return to the meadow…into the path of the monster. However, as she stepped away from the bush, Parsley, the rabbit stood in front of her.

"I will go; I can run a lot faster than you."

Before Liza could say anything, he was gone. She could hear him frantically calling Hazel's name.

❧❧❧

With his heart racing, Parsley ran into the long grass, calling at the top of his voice. In desperation he stood on his back legs and stared around. Suddenly, in the distance, he heard a small squeaky voice.

"Please help me, I'm lost."

Exhaling with relief, he cried. "Hold on, I'm coming." Following the sound of her voice, he saw Hazel huddled in a clump of grass. Wasting no time on ceremony, Parsley grabbed her by the scruff of the neck, and ran flat out to safety…the monster close on his heels. He could smell the fumes…hear the blades scything into the grass.

It was nearly on top of him, his lungs burned with the effort to out-run it. He reached the edge of the woods just in time, and skidded to a halt beside Liza. She was hysterical, crying with joy and gratitude.

Parsley dropped Hazel, and stood panting, trying to get his breath.

"Oh thank you, thank you," Liza cried, hugging Hazel close. "What can I say? I don't know how to thank you."

"Please," Parsley said, still struggling to catch his breath. "It was my pleasure, I'm glad I could help.

However, you need to get away from here. The monster will be close again soon." Turning away from the field, he led them into the woods. The quiet coolness calmed their nerves.

Parsley wanted to join his family, so he said goodbye and hopped away. "Stay safe," he called, as he disappeared among the trees.

శ్రీశ్రీశ్రీ

Liza and her family huddled together, trying to get over the shock of what was so nearly a disaster.

"I'm sorry mother," Hazel whimpered. "I couldn't keep up, I did try, honestly."

Liza couldn't help laughing as she kissed her little daughter. Her joy and relief were contagious, and soon the woods echoed to the sound of their laughter. Raising a paw, Liza wiped tears of laughter from her face and glanced around. A few feet from them stood an old tree, a little way up its trunk, she noticed a hole. "Come," she said, gathering the youngsters together. "We need to rest, follow me."

Their long claws scrabbled for purchase, as they followed her up the gnarled tree trunk to the hole. Inside it was empty and clean. A little moss, dead grass and a feather or two layered the bottom. The youngsters snuggled down; they were exhausted and glad to be together.

Liza sat at the entrance. After all the excitement, it would take her a while to unwind.

Sighing with contentment, she gave herself a good wash, before joining her sleeping youngsters. No sooner had she curled up, than she too was asleep, dreaming of the reunion with her father.

Liza had no idea how long she'd slept, but a strange noise had woken her. She sat up and listened. Her ears twitched to the strange sound.

Almond and Solo were also awake. "What's that noise mother?" They asked.

Before Liza could answer, they heard it again…a strangled howling sound. Cocking her head to the side, she listened. *It could it be a fox,* she thought. They heard it again and stared at each other. Liza frowned. *I don't think it's a fox.* Her mind went back to the farm and Zadock.

Glancing at Almond and Solo, she whispered, "It could be a dog."

Solo frowned. "Like the one that killed father?"

Liza nodded.

Hazel and Corsi stirred and looked up at her. Seeing Almond and Solo awake, they scrambled to their feet.

"What's wrong mother?" Corsi asked.

Liza could feel him trembling. "Nothing to worry us," Liza said, hoping they couldn't hear the nervous tremor in her voice. "Come now, we will eat, and then continue our journey."

Scrambling to the ground, they were pleased to see plenty of nuts around. Staying close to the base of the tree, in case of danger, they feasted. The delicious nuts quickly erased any memory of strangled cries.

When they finished eating, Liza led them deeper into the woods. It was dark now and she felt a little safer. Not far from the tree, they found a small stream, and enjoyed a much needed drink. They were all wary and alert, each one keeping an eye out for any danger.

Hazel stuck to her mother like glue.

After their drink they travelled on, pushing through dense undergrowth. After a while they came to the edge of a small clearing. They smelt him, before they saw him.

"Get down, and stay quiet," Liza hissed, unable to hide the tremor of fear in her voice.

His soft crying ceased when he saw them.

They stared at each other in silence. It was as though time stood still.

Chapter Eight

Chester stared at the rats. His body trembled with anticipation as a crazy thought entered his head. *Maybe, they will be willing to help me*. He knew if anyone could set him free, they could. Their teeth would make short work of the rope. A feeling of guilt overwhelmed him. He'd killed many rats in his time, and enjoyed it. Now he needed their help.

The rope around his neck was so tight, he could hardly breathe. He was desperately tired and thirsty. In a voice no more than a hoarse whisper, he asked. "Please would you help me?" Terrified of scaring them away, he lowered his head as much as he could, and gently wagged the tip of his tail.

Liza had turned sideways on, hoping to conceal her young ones from his view. With fluffed fur and twitching tail, she stared at him, her eyes blazing. For a brief moment they faced off in silence.

Whimpering softly, Chester struggled to stand on his shaky legs. His voice trembled with anxiety as he had one last go at convincing them to help him. "My master tied me to this tree. He intended to shoot me, but his new pup escaped and ran off after a rabbit. I believe my master has left me here to die." Chester sniffed as a hot tear trickled down his face.

"I've tried to bite through this rope, but I can't. Will you help me, I won't hurt you, I promise. Please believe me," his tear filled eyes pleaded with them.

Unsure what to do, Liza looked at her youngsters, and then back at Chester. *Can I trust him?* She could see the rope tied around the tree, so he was telling the truth about that. Tentatively, she stepped closer.

Chester held his breath, but his wagging tail sent the young ones scurrying backwards.

"Oh no, please," he cried. "I won't hurt you, don't leave me!"

His desperate rasping cries tore at Liza's heart. Huffing, she glanced at her youngsters.

"What shall we do mother?" Hazel asked.

Liza shook her head. "I don't know. He seems genuine."

The youngsters made it obvious they wanted to leave. Their frightened squeaks added to Liza's confusion. Twitching her tail, she told them to be quiet. Facing Chester, she said. "Why should we help you?"

He could hear the distrust and scorn in her voice. He knew there was no way he could convince her. He could only hope she would take pity on him, and give him a chance to prove himself. "Please help me," he said softly. "I give you my word; I will not harm you, or your young ones."

Sitting upright, with her front paws resting on her tummy, Liza studied him. For some reason she felt she could trust him.

The youngsters squealed, when they realised she was going to help him. "Don't go mother," they cried.

Liza could hear the fear in their voices, but ignored them.

Chester's heart raced as he watched her approach.

As Liza drew closer, she could see for herself where he'd tried to bite through the rope. Bits of shredded tree bark and dried blood were clear to see.

"I'm going to jump onto your back, and chew the rope from there, so keep still," she said. Leaping for his shoulder, she used his long fur to pull herself up. Once on his back, his coat was so long, she disappeared from sight.

Trembling, her youngsters crouched together, watching her.

Slowly, Liza crawled through his fur, until she was almost sitting on top of his head. Resting her front paws on the tree trunk, she gnawed at the rope.

Chester held his breath; he could hardly believe his luck. He knew she would have no trouble setting him free. There were no words to express his relief and gratitude. He stood still, listening to the comforting sound of her incredible teeth, making short work of the thick rope.

Suddenly, it was done, the rope fell apart, and he was free. With a deep sigh, Chester lowered his head. He winced at the stiffness in his neck and back. His shaky legs would no longer hold him. Collapsing to the ground, he rested his chin on his paws. "How can I ever thank you? Is there anything I can do for you? I am at your service."

As Liza scrambled to the ground, her eyes brightened. She realized she'd made a friend, and what a friend! This dog was old, but he was big and still strong. She could sense a plan formulating in her mind. She shook her head, in an effort to ground her thoughts. *First things first, he's weak and dehydrated. I must take him to water.*

"You must be thirsty," she said. "If you follow me, I'll take you to a nearby stream."

With a weary groan, Chester struggled to his feet and followed her.

With loud squeaks of fear; the youngsters tried to hide behind their mother.

Liza frowned. "For goodness sake, pull yourselves together! If he was going to kill me, I would be dead by now."

"Please believe me," Chester said softly. "I will never hurt any of you."

Liza led him to the small stream.

Crouching by the stream, Chester lapped the cold water. It slaked his thirst and soothed his raw throat. When he'd drunk his fill, he lay down to rest.

"What is your name?" Liza asked.

"Chester," the old dog replied, raising his weary head, he asked. "What are your names?"

After making the introduction, Liza sat beside him. She told him her story, how they were going back home, to live with her father. She told him how Zadock was killed by the farm dog.

For a moment, there was an awkward silence. Chester turned his head away; he didn't know what to say.

Liza took the opportunity to share her plan with him. "Could we travel together?"

To her relief, as he faced her, she could see a spark of interest in his eyes.

"I would be delighted," he said. "After all I have no plans. I'm alone and I've nowhere to go…it appears I'm unwanted."

Liza moved closer to him. "We want you," she said, glancing at her youngsters.

Chester smiled; delighted to have found some friends.

Deciding to take the bull by the horns, Liza blurted out. "If it's alright with you, maybe we could ride on your back. It would make the journey so much quicker." Lowering her eyes, she stared at him through her lashes. "I need to get home as soon as possible, as my father is old."

Chester could see the anxiety in her eyes. Gently, he touched her with his nose. "Don't worry; I'm more than happy to help. Please, jump on my back, and rest yourselves. I know the way, and can do the journey in half the time it will take you."

Wide eyed, the four youngsters stared at their mother.

"Come on," she said, "I trust him."

Chester grinned…thrilled to have company, even if it was five rats. "Don't be scared, climb aboard. You'll be safer on my back than on the ground." He flattened his body to make it easier for them.

Liza led the way; grabbing hold of his long coat, she hauled herself onto his neck, and settling between his shoulder blades.

Corsi the bravest did the same; he was quickly followed by Almond and Solo.

Little Hazel stared at them, unmoving, her feet firmly planted on terra firma.

"Come on Hazel," her siblings shouted. They were enjoying this new adventure.

Chester flattened himself still further. "Come on little one. Honestly, I mean you no harm. I owe your mother my life, please trust me."

Trembling, Hazel stared up at her mother.

Liza nodded and gave her a reassuring smile.

Tentatively, Hazel walked towards them. With enthusiastic encouragement from her siblings, she clambered onto Chester's back and huddled close to her mother.

"Right then, are we ready?" Chester asked. "Hide in my fur and hang on."

Little Hazel squeaked, as Chester rose to his feet and walked deeper into the woods.

His old body ached from the dreadful ordeal he'd been through, and hunger gnawed at his stomach.

Nevertheless, he was alive…no longer thirsty, and in the company of good friends.

Not only that, but now he had purpose…a reason to keep going. Out of the blue, his life was filled with hope. He felt a new spring in his step, he was free and he was happy.

He could feel the five warm bodies on his back, like little hot water bottles. He was on an adventure, and he was not alone, things were looking up. "There's life in the old dog yet," he said quietly to himself.

Chapter Nine

Chester padded slowly through the trees and thick foliage. He wanted to keep away from well used tracks, for fear of bumping into any humans out walking; or worse still, his master. "Ouch!" He suddenly yelped. "You're scratching my back." His complaint echoed in the stillness.

"Sorry," a chorus of voices replied. The youngsters had been awake for a while, nibbling his fur and playing. In the excitement, young Almond nearly fell off his back. In her effort to stay aboard, she'd dug her long nails into his skin.

Liza called them to order, and for a while they were quiet.

Grateful for Liza's intervention, Chester pushed on. Peering through the trees, he spotted a small clearing. Hurrying towards it, he slumped in the cool grass.

Liza and her family scrambled off his back. "I think we all need some food," she said. "And our friend here needs a rest."

Touched by her concern, Chester had to admit, he was tired. By traveling through the night, they'd put a few miles behind them. Chester gazed up at the sky. "Dawn is not far away, and from the look of the sky, we could be in for a storm. Will you be okay here, if I go and find myself some food?"

Glancing round, Liza smiled. "We will be fine. Hidden among these trees, no one will see us." There was an abundance of dandelion leaves. Her youngsters were already busy eating.

Chester chuckled as he left them tucking into a hearty breakfast. Realising, his own meal would not be so easily come by, his amusement faded. With his nose to the ground, he searched, hoping to catch the scent of something, anything he could eat.

He saw it, before he smelt it…pheasant! She was busy pecking at the ground with her back to him. He didn't enjoy pheasant much; they had a strong flavour, and could be tough. *Oh well, beggars can't be choosers,* he thought. *And at least they're easy to catch.*

Crouching close to the ground, his old hunting skills came into play as he crept towards her. In his time, he'd caught many pheasants, mostly for his master. He couldn't understand why humans enjoyed eating them. *Maybe it's because they'd poached the birds from some Lord's estate,* he thought with a smile. Seeing the bird move towards a clump of bushes brought him out of his reverie. Chester knew, if she disappeared in there, he would lose her. *It's now or never,* he thought. Summoning all his strength, he went for her.

The pheasant saw him and took flight, but it was too late! Chester leaped into the air, and grabbed a mouthful of tail feathers. Pulling her to the ground, he dispatched her with a bite to the neck. He was so hungry he tore at the flesh, while at the same time spitting out feathers. With his initial hunger satisfied, he picked up the remains and returned to Liza and the youngsters.

The little family were curled up inside a small hollow, at the base of an old oak tree. Liza hurried to greet him. "I'm so pleased to see you. We thought you'd left us."

Seeing her relief, Chester smiled and assured her it would never happen. "I promised I would take you home, and I will. Here," he said dropping the pheasant carcass on the ground. "Have some meat."

Resting on his haunches, Chester watched the rats finish off the remaining meat and chew on the bones. He noticed the two boys, Corsi and Solo particularly enjoyed it. So much so, they argued over a small bone. But before Liza could intervene, a loud clap of thunder sent them all scurrying for shelter.

No one had noticed how black the sky had become. Lightning flashed, bathing the woods in an eerie glow. It was dark as night, and yet it was early morning. The storm was right overhead. The lightning flashes were so close; it was as if someone was turning a light switch off and on.

Liza and her youngsters huddled together, deep inside the hollow tree.

Trembling, Chester crouched as close to them as he could. He hated storms, and this was a bad one.

A sound like an explosion, told them a tree had succumbed to the force of the storm, and crashed to the ground.

Chester panted and shook with fear.

Liza and her family huddled even closer together.

"What was that?" Hazel cried, trying to squirm under her mother's belly. The others tried to join her. Liza could feel their small bodies shaking, she did her best to quell her own fear, and reassure them.

The storm seemed never ending…rain fell like stair rods. Only the thick canopy of branches above their heads saved them from a thorough soaking. Gradually, to everyone's relief, the storm moved away, and all they could hear was a low rumbling in the distance.

Relieved, Chester stood and shook himself, giving everyone a small shower.

"Hey"! They protested.

Stretching his stiff legs, Chester chuckled to himself. He'd not been this happy, or felt so free in a long time. Spotting a puddle of rain water, he called them over. Relaxed, now the storm had passed, they all enjoyed a welcome drink.

"I think we should make a move soon," Liza said.

Chester agreed. "I'm ready when you are."

No sooner were the words out of his mouth, than little Hazel, once so nervous, was now the first to try and climb up his leg.

"Hang on youngster," he said lowering his body to the ground. The grass felt wet and cold on his tummy. He gave an involuntary shiver.

"Are you alright?" Liza asked.

Chester grinned, "I will be, when you're all on board and settled. This grass is wet."

"Oh dear," Liza said grabbing Almond by the scruff and dragging her onto his back.

"Ouch mother, what's the hurry?"

"Chester's getting cold, hurry up all of you."

Corsi and Solo raced each other, both boys leaping with ease onto Chester's back.

"Right, are we ready?" The old dog asked, as he scrambled to his feet. Raising his head, he sniffed the air. "It's going to be a warm day, so I'll stick to the overgrown paths. We need to keep out of sight as much as possible." He knew it would slow him down and make the journey more difficult, but it would be safer in the long run, and cooler in the shade of the trees.

146

Chester could tell by the silence and lack of activity on his back…Liza and her youngsters were asleep. *I must avoid low branches. I don't want to lose my little passengers.* His whiskered lips rose in a smile. *I've made some new friends, and I even managed to catch my own breakfast.* He chuckled softly. *There's life in the old dog yet.* Moving slowly, like a large grey shadow, he vanished among the trees.

By late afternoon, he'd reached the edge of the woods. In the distance, he could hear a dog barking. Chester's rumbling stomach told him he was hungry. "Not surprising," he muttered to himself. "It was dawn when I last ate." His passengers were quiet, so he guessed they were still asleep. He could feel them warm on his back, so he knew they were safe.

A cool breeze moved through his fur. Leaves rustled on the trees, he hoped it wouldn't wake them. He stood for a moment to get his bearings, instinct told him to turn left. *We're not far from Tamwood now, maybe a couple of miles.* Aware the journey was nearly over, Chester sighed. Lowering his head, he raised a paw and wiped moister from his eye. He'd grown fond of his small companions, and would miss them. He was relieved to be away from his master and free, but he had no idea what he would do, or where he would go.

Chester's tail drooped; he knew he was too old to survive for long on his own. *I can hardly move in with Liza and her ratty family.* His heart raced at the thought of being alone. His long pink tongue lolled out of the side of his mouth.

"Stay calm," he whispered to himself. Gradually, his heart slowed and his nervous panting eased. He knew it was best not to dwell on the future. He was alive, and for the moment…not alone.

Turning left, he walked onto the road, his long nails clicking on the tarmac.

Solo woke up and stretched. Clambering up Chester's neck, close to his ear, he asked. "Where are we? Where have all the trees gone?"

Turning his head, Chester smiled. "You'd best go back to your family, and hide in my fur. We don't want you to be seen, now do we?"

Hearing their voices, Liza woke up. "Are we nearly home?" She asked.

Chester explained, they were close, but unfortunately the rest of their journey was through open countryside, until they reached Tamwood. "As soon as I find somewhere safe, we'll stop. I need to eat."

"So do we," Liza said doing her best to quiet her hungry youngsters.

Continuing on, they came to a farm. Chester stood and looked down the long drive, unsure if it was safe. There didn't appear to be any one about. No dogs rushed up barking at him. He decided to risk it. His body cast a long shadow, as he made his way warily towards a large barn. The door was slightly ajar, so he squeezed inside. Everywhere was quiet and still, which seemed unusual. A couple of half wild cats swore at him, and fled.

Making his way to the rear of the barn, he found a dark corner and lay down.

Liza and her family scrambled to the ground, and had a good sniff around.

While they washed and groomed each other, Chester explained his plan. "We'll eat," he said. "There should be no trouble finding food on a farm. Then after a short rest, we'll continue the journey. It will be dark by then and safer."

Liza agreed; her dark eyes sparkled with happiness at the thought of getting home.

Chester left them in the barn, where there was plenty to eat. Cautiously, he made his way out to the farm yard. A cat hissed and swore at him, but he ignored her. Keeping in the shadows, he had a good sniff around.

A hen had laid an egg under a small pile of logs. Chester made short work of it, enjoying the silky yolk as it slipped down his throat. *That was a nice appetizer,* he thought. *Now I need the main course.*

There were plenty of chickens scratching around the yard, but he knew they would make a lot of noise if he chased them, so he walked on and kept looking. Rounding a corner he saw why the farm was so quiet. In the distance, the farmer and his dogs were moving a large flock of sheep from one field to another.

Chester wondered how long it would take them. He needed to eat and be gone before they got back, or there could be big trouble, especially for him. Cautiously, he walked round the side of a shed and saw the farm house. The building was in darkness…all was quiet.

The back door was open, so he crept inside, and found himself in the kitchen. The smells were wonderful. Large hams hung on hooks from an old beam in the ceiling. A fire blazed in the hearth.

Chester's nose twitched, saliva dribbled from his mouth. Licking his lips, he savoured the aroma of baking bread. There was no one about, but he could hear voices coming from another room.

Quickly, he scanned the kitchen, and to his delight he spotted a plate of sausages on the table, along with some eggs. Ignoring the eggs, he grabbed a mouthful of sausage, and raced back to the barn. His heart thudded like a drum in his chest. He expected to hear angry shouts behind him, but all was quiet.

Breathing hard, he ran to the dark corner where he'd left his friends. Dropping the sausages, he sat down to get his breath.

"What's that?" Solo asked, sniffing the meat with interest.

"They're called sausages," Chester explained. "Help yourselves, they're delicious."

There were plenty, and Chester was happy to share. They all tucked in, enjoying the sausage feast.

On his way back with the sausages, Chester had noticed a large water trough, so after finishing his meal, he crept out and had a refreshing drink.

Chapter Ten

Concealed by a bale of straw, Liza and her family waited for Chester to return. Liza's ears pricked at the sound of scurrying feet.

"What's that scratching sound, mother?" Hazel asked.

Liza's tail twitched with agitation. "Its rats," she said. "They won't welcome our presence in their territory, so stay close to me." Her eyes brightened with relief as Chester trotted over to them.

Licking the excess water off his whiskers, he lay down with a contented sigh. *I'll have a short doze.* Sensing their agitation, he opened one eye and peered at Liza. "What's the matter?"

Snuggling closer to him, she whispered. "Rats."

"Oh don't worry about them. You're safe with me." Resting his chin on his paws, he closed his eyes and dozed, one ear twitching to the nocturnal sounds.

As darkness settled over the farm, all was quiet, apart from cattle lowing in a nearby shed, and a few chickens scratching about on the floor of the barn.

Raising his head, Chester gazed into the darkness. Rising to his feet, he yawned, and stretched, his tired legs.

The chickens scattered, protesting loudly.

"Oh shush!" Chester grumbled.

Looking up at him, Liza voiced what he was thinking. "I suppose we should move on."

Chester nodded.

The youngsters were quiet for once, busy grooming each other, until Corsi got a bit rough and Solo squeaked in protest.

"Be quiet," Liza said.

"But he bit me mother."

"Don't be such a baby, I didn't mean it," Corsi said doing his usual strutting.

"Be quiet all of you, we're not safe here." Chester glanced at Liza. "Time to go," he said, with an enthusiasm he didn't feel.

Liza nodded and scrambled onto his back.

The youngsters followed, concealing themselves in his long fur.

Hazel went straight to her favourite place between his shoulder blades, and made herself comfy.

Chester had no idea this part of his anatomy was missing some fur, where Hazel had nibbled it short.

Once they were settled, Chester cautiously made his way out of the barn, and into the darkness. No one had seen them come...no one saw them leave. Reaching the end of the drive, Chester looked back. The lights of the farm house were on, a welcome sight in the darkness. He sighed, at the thought of a warm fire and a good dinner.

"Are you okay?" Liza asked, sensing the farm's pull on him.

"Fine," he replied wistfully, "Just looking."

Taking one last glance, he turned onto the road. He knew it would take them all the way to Tamwood. However, with a couple of large fields to cross, it was the long way, so he decided to cut through a small wood, which would save them some time. Having made his decision he set off down the road, the woods were only a mile or so further on. Apart from the rhythmic tapping of his nails on the tarmac, and the eerie hoot of an owl, all was quiet.

"Are you asleep?" He whispered to the rats curled up in his fur.

"No," they chorused.

Plodding on, Chester told them his plan. "It will cut a few miles off our journey, if we go through the woods."

"Are we nearly there, then?" Solo asked.

Chester smiled. "No not yet. Tamwood is on the other side of the fields, and your mother says her home is a little way through a small wood."

"That's right." Liza tried to control her excited trembling. Tamwood, the name conjured happy memories. How she longed to see her father, Soar and her sister, Seamist. She hadn't realized how much she'd missed them.

How grateful she was to Chester, and so glad she had set him free. Liza knew without him, they would not have made it, and if they had, she might have missed seeing her father. It pays to be kind she thought to herself. With an inaudible sigh of contentment, she curled up in Chester's fur with her young ones.

It was well past midnight and pitch black, when they turned off the road into a small wooded area.

"Hang on," Chester told them. "I can't avoid overhanging branches."

Snuggling down, the rats gripped his fur with their paws…excited more than afraid. However, when an owl hooted or a fox barked, Chester felt them stiffen; but a soft word of encouragement soon instilled confidence.

They were making good time, and dawn was only a few hours away. However, as they entered a small clearing, Chester suddenly yelped and sat down whimpering.

"What's the matter?" Liza asked clambering to the ground.

"Be careful." Chester cried. "There is glass everywhere, and a piece is in my paw."

"Oh dear, can I get it out?" Liza asked.

"I don't know." Chester offered her his paw.

Liza sighed. "It's too dark, and with so much fur round your paw, I can't see anything. Let's take a rest, it will be light soon, maybe I can get it out then," she encouraged, trying to hide the concern in her voice.

Careful to avoid the broken glass, they moved under a thick shrub to wait for dawn.

Chester licked and licked his paw, hoping to get the sliver of glass out, but it was in too deep. Already his pad was swelling and beginning to throb.

Concerned, Liza and the youngsters nestled close to him. It was their turn to encourage him.

Chester was grateful for their company…glad he was not alone. He hoped in the daylight, Liza might be able to see and get the glass out.

Gradually, the sun rose over the woods, its soft rays chasing away the shadows.

Liza gently touched Chester's leg. "I may be able to see now, let me have look."

Chester glanced at her, his eyes bright with hope as he turned his paw over.

"Can you get it out, mother?" Almond asked snuggling close to Chester.

Liza frowned. "I don't know. I will do my best." She could see the sliver of glass between two pads. It was in deep, with dried blood around it. Gently, she tried to separate the pads with her paws, so she could get at the glass with her teeth, but the pads were swollen, just touching them made him cry out. *This isn't good*, she thought.

Gazing sympathetically at Chester, she said. "I can't remove it."

Chester could see the concern in her eyes. Shaking his head, he said softly. "Don't worry."

Solo and Corsi stood together staring at him, "Does it hurt a lot?" Solo asked.

Chester nodded.

"So what will we do, if you can't walk?" Almond asked.

The youngsters gathered round their mother...frightened eyes fixed on Chester.

Seeing their concern, Chester gave what he hoped was a reassuring smile. "The first thing we do is get you all on my back. We need to get out of these woods. Now it's light, I can see where I am treading." Lowering his head, he gently nudged Almond with his nose. "Don't worry little one. It may take a bit longer, but we'll make it."

He limped so badly, young Hazel had to move from between his shoulder blades, and join the others in the middle of his back, or risk falling off.

It seemed to take forever, but eventually they made it out of the woods and found themselves in a large field. The sun was high in the sky promising a lovely day. A herd of grazing cows looked up as they came into view. One or two were curious and wanted to know what was wrong.

Chester explained about the glass in his paw.

Liza and her family kept a low profile, hidden from sight in his long fur.

The cows were sympathetic to Chester's plight, and told him their farm was not far away. "Our farmer will help you," they assured him.

Chester thanked them and slowly limped on, following the edge of the field.

Overhead a large wood pigeon circled above them, its mournful cry drifting on the morning air.

Liza's ears pricked up at the sound. *I know that voice, I'm sure I do.* All of a sudden it came to her. "That's Seed!" She exclaimed. "I'm sure it is."

"What seed mother, where?" Solo asked. His body trembled with anticipation.

Almond nudged her mother. "I'm hungry, can I have some seed?"

Liza smiled. "No! No! Seed is a pigeon. She is a friend to us rats. I'm sure that's her flying above us." Pushing Chester's thick fur aside, Liza's eyes narrowed with frustration as she peered up. *How can I get her attention?* A thought came to her. Scrambling towards Chester's neck, she asked. "Can you see that pigeon?"

"I can," he replied.

Liza's tail twitched with excitement. "Bark at it, please. Do anything you can to get her attention."

Raising his head, Chester barked; "Hey, you there!"

The Pigeon heard him, and slowly circled to the ground, landing heavily a few feet from them.

It has to be Seed, Liza thought. *No other pigeon crash lands like her.*

The bird strutted over to them. "What's all the noise about?" She asked her head to one side.

"Is your name Seed?" Chester asked.

"Who wants to know?"

"There's someone here who wants to talk to you." He slumped in the grass, grateful to rest his paw.

The pigeon's head bobbed nonstop, as she stared at him. "I don't see anyone," she said glancing around.

Unable to contain herself any longer, Liza scrambled off Chester's back, and cried. "Seed, it's me Liza, King Flylord's daughter."

Seed's feathered brow rose in amazement. "Oh my, oh my," she said strutting closer and peering hard at Liza. "My goodness, it is you. How you've changed my dear." Noticing the youngsters, still hiding in Chester's fur, she exclaimed. "What's this I see?"

"These are my kittens," Liza explained, introducing them all by name.

"My goodness, this is a surprise. Come down little ones, let me look at you, don't be shy."

As usual, Corsi led the way, quickly followed by Solo and Almond. Hazel brought up the rear, standing as close to her sister as she could. Wide eyed the youngsters stared at the large plump pigeon.

Liza gazed proudly at them, as she told Seed they were making their way home. Briefly she explained how they had met Chester, and about their journey so far.

Seed's head bobbed back and forth as she listened.

Watching her, the youngsters tried not to giggle.

Liza finished her story, took a deep breath and sat down.

Seed cooed with amazement, her round eyes widened. "I've been visiting with my cousin, and was about to fly home," she explained. "I'm so glad I was late leaving, or I would have missed you." Fluffing her feathers, she raised her head. "I live in the woods near Optimus now, you know," she said proudly.

Moving closer to Liza, she gazed down at her. "Oh my dear, I am so thrilled to see you. I can't tell you how concerned we've been. Your dear father the king has grown old, and sadly his back legs have become weak, nevertheless his spirit is strong." Tilting her head to the side, she gazed at Liza. "He misses you terribly, we all do."

For a moment, Liza thought she could see a tear in the pigeon's eye. In a tremulous voice she asked. "What about my brother, Soar?"

Seed rose to her full height and smiled. "Ah, your brother, he is well, and has grown in wisdom and stature; a fine young prince indeed. But listen to me waffling on. You must be so eager to get home. I know they'll all be thrilled to see you."

"Do you really think so?" Lowering her head, Liza stared at the ground.

"Oh my dear, don't ever doubt it." Seed wished she could hug her, she looked so sad and vulnerable. She glanced at Chester. "Nice to meet you, young man," she said with a twinkle in her eye. "Thank you for looking after this little family."

"It has been my pleasure," Chester replied. Chuffed at being called a young man, he decided he liked this chubby pigeon.

Seed's voice brimmed with confidence as she called them to order. "Now, let's see if we can sort this situation out. It's obvious to me, Chester needs help with his paw, while Liza and her family want to get home." The old bird's head bobbed back and forth, as she tried to get to grips with the situation.

Raising a wing, she cooed. "I have an idea. Not far from here, there's a farm. The humans are kind people. Mind you, they have tried to shoot me on occasion." Her frown softened into a smile, as she turned to Chester. "Nevertheless, I'm sure they will help you. Once we reach the farm, it's no distance to Lisa's home, Tamwood. I would be honoured to help you all." She stared at their expectant faces.

"What's your plan?" Chester asked.

Happy to have his attention, she quickly shared her idea. "If I take you to the farm, I'm sure the humans will help you, and let you stay with them. Then I will guide Liza and her little ones, the rest of the way home." Chuffed with herself, she gazed round at them. "What do you think?"

Chester and Liza agreed, her plan was good, and decided to make tracks right away. Wasting no time, Liza and her young ones, scrambled onto Chester's back.

Seed took to the air, shouting enthusiastically. "Follow me!"

Chester's paw throbbed with pain, but he couldn't help smiling at the old bird. She was eccentric, but likable. Trying to keep his swollen paw off the ground, he bravely limped after her.

Seed flew low, shouting occasional words of encouragement, and cooing happily to herself.

Chapter Eleven

Fortunately for Chester, the farm was no great distance. Nevertheless, struggling on three legs took its toll…sapped his strength. Every time his paw touched the ground, he winced with pain. Exhausted and thirsty, he was forced to stop a number of times to rest. "I wish I could have a drink," he said quietly. Licking his dry lips, he plodded on.

Liza heard him and sighed. *I wish I could do something to help him. I just hope we reach the farm soon, he can't go much further.*

As if reading her thoughts, Seed called out. "Here we are my dears, nearly there."

Rounding a corner they saw the farm up ahead. Bathed in sunshine, it was a welcome sight.

Sighing with relief, Chester sat down, glad of a chance to rest his paw.

A farm dog saw them and barked a greeting.

"We'd best get down and hide," Liza said. Once on the ground, Liza, and her youngsters stood in front of Chester. Staring into his eyes they were overcome with gratitude.

"Will you be alright?" Hazel asked tearfully, as she stared up at his shaggy old face.

"We will miss you," they all said in unison.

Lowering his head, Chester smiled. "Don't worry about me, I'll be fine." He turned to Liza. "Get home safely; and thank you for saving my life. I will never forget any of you." Tears filled the old dog's eyes. "If there is ever anything I can do for you, just let me know. As long as I live, I am your friend."

Standing on her hind legs, Liza reached for his lowered head. Her small paws gently touched his nose.

They stared at each other, words were unnecessary.

Perched in a tree above them; Seed's heart ached with emotion, as she watched the sad farewell.

Turning away, Liza led her small family under a bush, where they would be safe, but could see the farm clearly.

Barking with excitement, the farm dog trotted up to Chester. Still very much a pup, she was thrilled to see another dog. Wagging her tail, she rolled playfully onto her back, poking at him with her feet, eager to be friends.

Chester winced, as she touched his swollen paw.

"Oh I'm sorry, are you hurt?" Scrambling to her feet she stared at him.

Raising his paw, Chester told her about the glass. "I've tried, but I can't get it out."

"Don't worry; come with me, my humans will help you." She led him towards the farm.

Slowly, Chester followed her. Briefly, he stopped and looked back at the rats hiding under the bush. "Goodbye," he mouthed, before turning and limping after the pup.

"What's your name?" The pup asked.

"They call me, Chester."

"My name's Milly. My master is teaching me to herd sheep. He says my mother is the best. She's won lots of trophies. But my master says I will be as good as her one day."

Chester smiled, the pups animated chatter kept his mind off his throbbing paw. Nevertheless, anxiety made his empty stomach churn. He paused for a moment, his eyes narrowed with concern. "Are you sure your master will help me?"

Seeing the fear in his eyes, Milly gently touched his nose with hers. "Of course they will; my humans love dogs." Swinging round, she bounced ahead of him, her tail going ten to the dozen.

I hope you're right, Chester thought. His tail drooped between his legs as he limped after her.

Liza and the young ones watched.

"Will he be alright mother?" Almond asked.

"I miss him already," Hazel said tearfully.

"Maybe it's a trap!" Solo and Corsi said, staring at their mother with wide eyes.

Liza smiled at them. "Don't be silly, he'll be fine. I'm sure he will." Liza desperately hoped her optimism wasn't misplaced. Her long tail twitched, as she watched Milly lead Chester to the farmhouse door, and stand there barking. Her heart raced when a tall woman appeared at the door.

"What's happening mother?" The youngsters asked.

Perched on her back legs, Liza could see more clearly. Seeing the woman bend down and pat Chester on the head. She released the breath she didn't realise she'd been holding. "It's alright," she said. "The woman has taken Chester inside the house. He's safe now."

☙☙☙

"Indeed he is," Seed cooed. Fluttering to the ground, she encouraged them out from under the hedge. "We'd best be going; the day will be over soon." Taking to the air, she called, "Follow me."

Flying low, Seed led them away from the farm, and out into a small meadow.

Liza's heart skipped a beat, she knew Tamwood forest was on the other side of the meadow…home territory. With renewed confidence, she urged the youngsters to hurry and follow her.

Seed sighed with impatience. At this pace, it will take for ever to reach the forest. Nevertheless, she did her best to encourage them. "It's not far now," she called. Flying low, she kept a look out for trouble. She could only just see them, running through the long grass. *They're vulnerable now, without their friend Chester,* she thought. Tutting to herself, she skimmed low over the ground. "He brought them safely this far, I don't want anything bad to happen to them; not on my watch!"

The long meadow grass afforded the rats some cover. Nevertheless, to Seed, it seemed to take forever, before the little group reached the relative safety of the woods.

Huddled under a bush, Liza and her young ones regrouped and took a much needed rest.

"Stay here, and don't move," Seed told them. "I will be back shortly." Launching into the air, she disappeared among the trees.

"Where's she going?" Almond asked.

Hazel snuggled closer to Liza. "I'm frightened mother."

"Hazel's a scaredy rat," Corsi said scrambling over his brother to taunt her.

Solo pushed him off with a squeak of protest.

"Be quiet, all of you," Liza hissed. "We wait here, until Seed returns."

"But what if she doesn't come back mother?" Hazel asked.

Trying to ignore her churning stomach, Liza snuggled down. "She'll return," she said softly, hoping they couldn't hear the anxiety in her voice.

⊰⊰⊰

Seed skimmed through the forest, her bright eyes darting everywhere. Eventually, she spotted what she was looking for…her friend the Blackbird. Perching on a branch beside him, she fluffed her feathers and bobbed her head. "I need a favour," she said moving closer to him.

The bird glanced at her, "What favour?"

"Do you know King Flylord?"

The Blackbird nodded. "Of course, everyone knows him, why?"

Hardly drawing breath, Seed told him about Liza and her young ones.

The Blackbird's yellow beak dropped open as he listened.

"They are returning home," Seed explained. "Would you give King Flylord the message?"

"How wonderful, I will go right away."

Seed thanked him, and made her way back to Liza. Perching on a low branch, she watched them enjoying a meal of nuts, and dandelion leaves. "Are we ready to move on then?"

Her sudden appearance took them by surprise. They bunched together staring at her.

"You came back," Liza said.

Seeing Liza's relieved expression, Seed smiled. "Of course; I said I would." Cocking her head to the side, she gazed at their expectant faces. "So, if you're ready? Follow me."

Almond trotted beside her mother. "Is it much further now?"

Liza's heart skipped a beat as she thought about seeing her family again. She smiled at Almond. "No, it's not far now. Soon you will meet your grandfather."

"Ooh, will he like us mother, will he?" Corsi and Solo trembled with excitement.

Little Hazel squeaked with impatience. "Of course he will. He's our grandfather."

Liza chuckled, delighted to see her young daughters surprising boldness. *So much for being the runt of the litter*, she thought. *Watch out world, here comes, Hazel!*

Hazel glanced at her mother. "What?" She asked.

"Nothing little one," Liza's eyes twinkled as she encouraged them to hurry. "Your grandfather will love you all, so don't be afraid. Now come on, we must keep Seed in sight. We will be home soon." Her heart fluttered pleasantly, as she said the word home; her whole being felt strangely stirred.

Corsi stared intently at her. "Mother, are you alright?"

"Yes, my son, I'm fine. I just want to see my father, that's all."

Seed flew from branch to branch, making sure they could always see her. She called and cooed, encouraging them to keep moving. Through the trees, she could see the sun's fiery rays as it dropped below the horizon. *I must get them to King Flylord, before night falls.*

They making good time, when all of a sudden, Almond's loud cry brought them to a shuddering halt. She was at the rear of the small party, trotting behind Solo, while Hazel, and Corsi, stuck close to Liza. They all swung round, fearful of what they might see.

Fearing the worst, Liza ran to Almond. "What is it? What's wrong?"

"I saw something mother, it was awful...like needles moving, over there." Almond raised a paw and pointed, her eyes searched the darkness for the moving needles.

Seed flew down, curious as to the hold up. "What's the matter?"

"Almond saw needles, moving," Liza explained. "What could it be?"

Seed chuckled. "It's probably a hedgehog."

"What's that?" Solo asked. Seed looked at him, a wicked glint in her small dark eyes. "Like a rat, but with needles instead of fur." She burst out laughing.

"That's not funny, or true," a voice said from the darkness.

They all stared intently, as a small brown creature came out of the bushes and waddled towards them. It had bright dark eyes, a shiny black nose, and sharp spines all over its back.

Liza and the youngsters froze their eyes wide in amazement. However, when the first was joined by a second, that was too much for Hazel and Almond, their loud squeals of panic echoed through the trees.

Seed, realizing the situation was getting out of control, flapped her wings, in an attempt to draw attention away from the two hedgehogs. "Calm down! They mean you no harm," she shouted.

Liza came to her senses and shook her head. She remembered seeing hedgehogs when she was young. "Seed is right, so quiet down. All this noise will attract the attention of predators."

The two hedgehogs were quite bemused by the effect they were having. Normally, they were the ones getting into a panic, and rolling into a tight ball for safety. The first hedgehog decided to introduce himself. "Hello, my name's Prickle, and this, is my sister Bramble."

Liza and Seed introduced themselves, but the four youngsters continued to stare open mouthed.

Seed shook her head and tutted. "Have you lost your voices, all of a sudden? Stop catching flies, and say hello."

The youngsters closed their mouths, and whispered in unison. "Hello."

The two hedgehogs smiled, and continued their search for food…melting like shadows into the darkness.

"Are they rats' mother? They don't look like us." Corsi whispered.

Liza shook her head. "No son, they are nothing to do with us." The blatant look of relief on his face made her smile.

Calmness restored, they regrouped and continued on their way keeping a close eye on Seed.

The pigeon sighed; relieved they were on the last leg of the journey. *We're so close now,* she thought. *If my friend the Blackbird has done what I asked, Liza's family should be aware we are coming.*

Alighting on a branch, she waited for the rats to catch her up. Glancing down, she watched Liza lead her youngsters through the long grass. Cocking her head to the side, she smiled. *Hopefully, they have a pleasant surprise waiting for them.*

Chapter Twelve

Thrilled to be the bearer of good news, the Blackbird flew as fast as he could. It was dark when he arrived at King Flylord's den. Most of the residents were up and about, foraging for food. Perching on a low branch nearby, he uttered the loud warning call only a Blackbird can make.

A couple of large bucks, searching for their supper looked up.

"What do you want?" One of them asked.

"I need to speak to your king. I have urgent news for him."

The two bucks looked at each other. The king was weak, could they risk disturbing him?

"What is your news?" The larger buck asked.

"My news is for the King's ears only. However, I will tell you this. It will make him happy."

"Very well, wait here and I will fetch him." The larger buck waddled off, leaving his friend with the Blackbird.

After a while, he returned, followed by a large frail looking rat. A number of young bucks milled around the King, ready to defend him should the need arise.

Standing on shaky legs, the King squinted up at the Blackbird. "What is it you wish to tell me?" He demanded, in a voice surprisingly strong, considering his frail condition.

"Your Highness," the Blackbird said, bowing his head. "Seed, the pigeon, has sent me to tell you that your daughter, Princess Liza is making her way home as we speak. Seed is leading them and they are close."

The king's mouth dropped open; he could hardly believe what he was hearing.

A murmur of delight went up from the assembled rats around the king.

Raising a paw, King Flylord brushed a tear from his eye. For a moment he could hardly speak. "This is indeed wonderful news," he eventually managed to say.

The Blackbird hopped to the ground and moved closer to the King.

Flylord peered at him. "You say Seed is leading them, who else is with my daughter?"

The Blackbird's heart fluttered with excitement. He knew what he was about to share, would bring the old King great joy. Taking a deep breath, he blurted out. "Princess Liza has young ones your highness, four to be exact, two bucks, and two does. It seems they've had quite an adventure, and will have much to tell you when they arrive."

Flylord's eyes widened as he stared at the Blackbird. "Young ones," he said softly.

The Blackbird nodded and smiled…delighted his news appeared to give the old king a new lease of life.

"This is wonderful! We must get the family together," the King exclaimed. "My daughter must have a welcome home party." He turned to the excited rats around him. "Go and find Prince Soar, and the rest of my family. Tell them to come to my chamber. The rest of you arrange refreshments. We will give her a homecoming befitting a Princess of this clan." Tears of joy pooled in the king's eyes. "My daughter is returning to us," he said softly. Turning to the Blackbird, he smiled. "Thank you for bringing me this great news. How long do you think they will be?"

"I'm not sure, your Highness, maybe an hour."

"Good," Flylord said. "That gives us plenty of time to arrange things." Before returning to the den, he invited the Blackbird to stay for the party.

"Thank you, Your Highness, I would be honoured."

ക%ക

Seamist and Malar were busy in the den, when the buck found them and told them of Liza's imminent return.

Sitting on her haunches, Seamist sighed with delight and rubbed her paws together. She knew Liza had always been a little jealous of her, nevertheless she had a genuine soft spot for her half-sister. "I'm so pleased she's coming home," she said to Malar, as they made their way to the King's chamber. "I know father has missed her. He's tried not to worry, but it's not been easy for him. This news will do him good, I am sure."

Malar, made no reply.

Seamist could see the concern on his face. His silence troubled her.

"What is it?" She asked. "You look worried."

Not wishing to burst her bubble, Malar said softly. "I hope she won't cause trouble, and is willing to settle down."

Seamist looked at him, a gentle smile on her face. "Do you really think she would succeed, if that's what she has come back to do." Halting for a moment, she took Malar's face between her paws and stared into his

171

eyes. "We are all changed, Malar, our lives are not the same anymore; you know that." Her eyes narrowed as she murmured. "I believe Zadock was the real problem, and there was no mention of him returning with her." She paused and her expression brightened.

"What happened to Soar, everything he's learned, he has passed on to us. It's like the ripples in a pond, touching all our lives…changing us for ever. If Liza is willing to accept that and embrace it, then she will find love and happiness here, with us, her family. I am sure that's what she wants."

When they arrived at King Flylord's chamber, they found him washing his tail and humming softly. He glanced up as they entered. "I need to look my best," he said.

Seamist went to him, and kissed his cheek. "I'm so happy for you father. It will be lovely to see her again."

Flylord smiled fondly at his daughter. "Thank you my dear, I can hardly wait to see her. She has four little ones you know."

Seamist's heart skipped a beat at the news. She was delighted for Liza, and knew from experience; having babies forces one to grow up, and be responsible.

"Is there anything you need us to do sir?" Malar asked.

Before the king could answer, Prince Soar, Pecan, and three of their older youngsters, entered the chamber.

"This is wonderful news, father," Prince Soar exclaimed. "We are delighted."

"Indeed we are," Pecan said, as she ran over to Seamist, followed by her excited youngsters.

Now the family was together, the king explained what he would like to do for Liza. "We haven't much time; she will be here soon." Smiling, he glanced at each one. "I would like the den to appear empty, so that when she arrives, we can surprise her. I've sent some bucks off to arrange food for a buffet. I think a welcome home party, would be nice don't you?" Encouraged by their delighted grins and enthusiastic nods, he rose to his feet.

Pecan's youngsters were not sure what was going on, but at the word party, they ran around squeaking with excitement.

In the atmosphere of joy and anticipation, King Flylord felt strangely rejuvenated. "There is something I would like you to do for me," he said.

Soar sat beside him. "Tell us, father. If it is possible, we will do it."

Reaching out a paw, Flylord gently touched his son's shoulder. "After the party when everyone has had time to rest. I would like Optimus to arrange a meeting at the Council Clearing.

"It would please me, if King Ludus, and King Pierro, could be here with us. I'm sure they would like to welcome Liza and her young ones home. It would be good to be united again as one great family."

Pausing, he stared at the ground, as a thought entered his head…a thought he would keep to himself until later.

Soar raised a brow, but nodded assent. "I will organise it, father, don't worry."

"Good, now let us prepare for the return of my daughter."

173

And so the welcome home party was arranged, with lots of delicious food laid on. Everyone went into hiding, waiting with eager anticipation for Liza to arrive.

Even the Blackbird was caught up in the excitement.

Chapter Thirteen

Seed arrived at the den a little ahead of Liza. Perching on a branch, her wings fluttered with anxiety. *Where is everyone? Surely the Blackbird brought my message.* Her eyes narrowed with concern. "Oh dear," she muttered to herself. Turning this way and that, she searched for the Blackbird, but he was nowhere in sight. Seed had no idea he was hiding, concealed under a canopy of leaves.

Just then Liza arrived. Seed watched the youngsters huddle close to their mother. They were breathing heavily, and trembling with anxiety.

Liza looked up at Seed. "Where is everyone?" She whispered. "I hope nothing is wrong."

Seed was about to answer her, when excited voices echoed all around them.

"Surprise!" They shouted.

Liza's mouth dropped open, as she watched her father, and the rest of the family come out of hiding.

"Welcome home, my child, and welcome to your little ones." Tears glistened in the old King's eyes as he shuffled towards her.

The other rats parted, letting him through.

Liza's heart raced as she ran to him. "Father, oh father! I've missed you so much." Snuggling close to him, she swallowed hard as she felt the frailty of his body. Resting her head on his shoulder, she sighed with relief. *At least he's still alive.* Kissing his cheek, she said softly. "I'm so sorry for the way I've behaved."

Flylord smiled. "It's alright Liza. I'm glad you're home safe. I've missed you so much." He glanced round at the others. "We all have."

The family milled around, laughing and talking as they welcomed her home.

The youngsters stood near Seed, their eyes widening as they watched.

King Flylord noticed them. "Are these your young ones?"

Liza nodded.

Moving towards them, Flylord said gently. "Come, let me look at you."

Trembling, they stood in front of him.

Corsi and Solo stood tall in an effort to hide their apprehension.

Hazel and Almond huddled together, quite overcome by it all. Seeing their grandfather the King, for the first time, along with so many other rats, was too much to cope with.

Their muted squeaks, made the King smile. Sitting on his haunches, he raised his paws. "Don't be afraid. Tell me your names."

Bowing their heads, Corsi and Solo introduced themselves.

Hazel and Almond stared open mouthed at him.

Liza chuckled. "Girls, this is your grandfather, you have nothing to fear. Tell him your names."

Glancing at her mother, Almond opened her mouth to speak, but the only sound to emerge was a strangled squeak.

Hazel stood on trembling legs, her eyes glued to her grandfather.

With an amused shake of her head, Liza stepped between them. Placing a gentle paw on each one, she introduced them to her father and all the other rats standing around.

Once the introductions were made, the youngsters seemed able to relax, and soon wandered off to play with the other young ones in the den.

King Flylord took Liza aside. "You have fine kittens, Liza. But tell me, who is their father? Is it Zadock? If so, where is he?"

Raising a paw, Liza brushed a tear from her eye. She shuddered, as the image of Zadock being shaken by the terrier, rose in her memory. Gazing into her father's face...seeing the concern in his eyes, she said softly. "Zadock is dead, killed by a terrier. I was left to rear our kittens alone."

King Flylord moved closer, and tried to comfort her.

Even so, Liza couldn't help noticing the relief in her father's eyes on hearing of Zadock's death. It saddened her, but she continued with her story. "I knew I couldn't stay there on my own, I needed to come home. So once my kittens were strong enough, we began our journey."

Shaking his head, King Flylord stared at her.

Seeing the admiration in his eyes, Liza nuzzled him. "I had no choice," she said softly. "I knew if we stayed, we would die."

Resting in the grass, Flylord listened as she told him about Chester, the old sheep dog. "His master had tied him to a tree and left him to die," she said in a choked voice. "I gnawed through the rope, and released him."

"My goodness," King Flylord gasped. "Why would you take such a risk?"

Liza shrugged her shoulders. "I don't know…somehow I knew I could trust him. He turned out to be a wonderful friend," she said softly. "He let us ride on his back, concealed in his fur. We would never have made it, without his help." Thinking about him, brought tears to her eyes. *I wish he could see us now, back home and safe.*

She went on to tell her father, how Chester stepped on broken glass, and got a sliver in his paw. "It caused him a great deal of pain, and I knew he couldn't go much further, but that's when we met up with Seed, the pigeon, which was a miracle!"

Liza smiled, as she explained how Seed led them to a farm, where Chester was able to get help with his paw. "We left him there, and followed Seed the rest of the way home."

While she was talking, Soar joined them. He sat amazed as he listened. "Wow!" He said. "That is some story; it almost makes my experience with the Rat Run a non-event.

Liza stared at him, open mouthed. "Don't ever say that! What I did was natural; I just wanted to come home. What you did was special. You could have refused to do it, but you didn't. You were willing to sacrifice your life for all of us; for lasting unity. I appreciate that now, and I understand."

Soar stared at his sister, she had changed in many ways, and it pleased him.

Liza held his intense gaze. She remembered how small and fragile he used to be; yet now, as he sat next to their father, he appeared to have grown. Even in the darkness, she felt drawn to him; somehow his presence gave her confidence.

Seamist, and Pecan, joined them. "It is good, to have you back with us Liza," they both said.

Overcome, by the love and acceptance she'd received from everyone, Liza dropped her head. "Thank you," she said softly.

"You must be tired my dear," Flylord said. "Seamist will show you where you can rest."

"Thank you father, I must confess, I do feel weary." Bowing her head in respect, she left him and rounded up her youngsters. Their loud protests…intermingled with yawns, made her smile as they followed Seamist to a cosy chamber in the den. Breathing a sigh of relief, Liza drew her little family round her, and they were soon asleep, relaxed in the knowledge they were home and safe.

∽∽∽

King Flylord sat beside Soar watching the members of his family, his clan. They were larger in number than ever before and all fine healthy rats. *This is what I always wanted*, he thought. *Peace…no more kidnap and violence.* His eyebrows drew together as he tried to remember a teaching from the book of wisdom. His eyes brightened as the words entered his mind. "Nothing is achieved by violence," he said softly. *We are certainly achieving more since the Rat Run, than we ever did in the past. Soar has taught us well.* Smiling, he glanced proudly at his son. *When I go, I will go happy, knowing my family…my clan, are in good and wise hands.*

Seeing tears in his father's eyes, Soar moved closer to him, and gently groomed his neck.

The old king ground his teeth in contentment. Lying down next to Soar, he listened to the happy sounds coming from the many young ones that now made up his family.

"I'm a blessed old rat," he muttered softly. Snuggling down, he enjoyed the warmth of his son's body.

Soar glanced at him. "What did you say, father?"

"Nothing, my son, I'm just happy." With a contented sigh, he closed his eyes and dozed, safe in the bosom of his family.

Chapter Fourteen

Seed the pigeon, having enjoyed King Flylord's hospitality, was, at his behest, flying through the night sky, on a mission to see Optimus the owl. She could still hear the agitation in the King's voice, as he'd told her to ask Optimus to arrange a meeting at the Council Clearing. "Tell him, it's urgent, as I need to inform King Ludus, and King Pierro."

Seeing the anxious twitch of his tail, Seed had smiled reassuringly. "Don't worry Your Highness, I will tell him."

"Good," Flylord said. "Once everyone is here, Liza's home coming will be official."

Flying high, Seed shook her head as she negotiated a narrow gap between a stand of tall Birch trees. Her bright beady eyes narrowed, as she mulled over their conversation. *The King has something else on his mind,* she thought. *Something he wants to share at the meeting. I wonder if it has something to do with Liza.*

Another thought filled her mind, as she drew close to the woods where Optimus lived. She shivered slightly, as she recalled the last time she'd made this journey. "How traumatic it was," she muttered to herself. Tutting, she tried to block the memory of Princess Shamrock's kidnap, and the resultant injuries and deaths.

Gazing down, she could see the clearing through the canopy of branches. Every muscle ached with exhaustion; nevertheless this time she was the bearer of good news. A lost daughter had returned home, and it was time to celebrate. A surge of happiness, gave Seed extra stamina.

Below her, bathed in moonlight, she saw the great oak standing proudly in the centre of the clearing. Fluttering down, she perched on a branch, and called to Optimus. There was no reply. "Oh dear, I hope he's home."

A soft breeze ruffled her feathers and she glanced up. Optimus the great owl was on a branch above her head. He fixed her with his large yellow eyes. "What can I do for you this time?"

Seed sighed with relief. "King Flylord has sent me. He politely requests a meeting to be arranged at the Council Clearing."

"And why would I do that?" Optimus said turning his head almost full circle; before giving her his undivided attention.

Fixed in his hypnotic stare, Seed's voice faltered slightly as she said. "It's wonderful news, King Flylord's daughter Princess Liza, has come home." Seeing the satisfied smile on the great owl's face, Seed relaxed. Although her heart raced a bit, as he flew down and perched next to her.

"Well, well! That is good news. I knew she would return. How is she? I imagine she has young ones with her."

Seed stared at him, wide eyed. *How does he always seem to know everything?*

Optimus could see the admiration in her eyes. Raising his feathered brows, he indicated she should continue.

Flustered, Seed bobbed her head. "Oh sorry. To answer your question, Liza is well, and you are right, she does have youngsters, two does, and two bucks. She has changed a lot."

The old owl smiled. "I am so pleased for her father. Wonderful news, and just in time I think. Return and tell him, the arrangements will be made. I will make sure King Ludus, and King Pierro, are informed. The meeting will be in two days' time, when the moon is full."

Once Seed had departed, Optimus wasted no time. He dispatched rooks to King Pierro, and King Ludus with the message that King Flylord's daughter had returned home and a meeting would be held at the Council Clearing in two days.

෴෴෴

Seed's heart fluttered with excitement as she rose into the sky. Soft fingers of light rose above the horizon, soon the early risers in the bird world, would sing a song of welcome to the dawn.

When she arrived at King Flylord's den, he was waiting with eager anticipation. As Seed gave him the message from Optimus, she couldn't help smiling. His delight and relief were obvious.

"Please stay and rest."

Seed gratefully accepted. Her head bobbed as she thanked the King. "It has been a long night, and I confess I am rather tired."

"Then stay with us," the King insisted.

A tall tree overlooked the den. Seed fluttered onto a branch, and made herself comfortable. A thick canopy of leaves made a cosy shelter, and in no time she was asleep.

At King Pierro's den, the news was received with delight. Pierro was thrilled for King Flylord, and glad of the chance to see his two sons, Piper, and Malar again.

Piper had chosen to live with Princess Shamrock and her father King Ludus. King Pierro missed him, but consoled himself with the fact that soon, some of Piper's young ones would be coming to live with their grandfather.

Pierro looked forward to that day with great anticipation. Old Bluebear had died, and King Pierro himself was not getting any younger, so to have young ones around the place would be most welcome.

Dear old aunty Freckle had also passed away. Pierro missed her, but smiled to himself, as he remembered how much she loved the young ones. *At least she died peacefully in her chamber. I must tell Piper and Malar when I see them.*

King Pierro had to choose who would accompany him to the Council Clearing. After much consideration, he chose Rupert and his young son Inky.

Inky, a fine variegated buck, was the spitting image of his father.

Both father and son were delighted to have the privilege of accompanying their King on such an auspicious occasion.

Inky's mother, Crystal, the little white doe, who'd been kidnapped, along with princess Shamrock, bade them both a tearful farewell.

"Stay safe," she said wrapping her paws around Inky's neck. She could feel him trembling with excitement.

Huffing with embarrassment, Inky pulled away. "I will be fine mother, don't fuss."

Crystal smiled. "I know, but this is a great honour, so listen to your father."

"I will," he replied as he hurried to his father's side.

Sitting up, and using her tail to balance, Crystal watched them leave. "Goodbye," she called. Raising a paw, she waved until they vanished in the undergrowth.

❧❧❧

In Athston, King Ludus hummed to himself as he made preparations to leave for the Council Clearing. He'd decided to take Piper and Shamrock, and a few of their young ones with him. The youngsters skipped about with excitement, they couldn't wait to get going

Outside the den a large rook waited patiently to guide them.

The journey went well, and they arrived safely at the Clearing.

The other clans arrived at pretty much the same time. They were all delighted to be together again.

Prince Soar greeted the Kings, and they chatted briefly.

Optimus stood like a large grey ghost, watching the proceedings.

They were all genuinely thrilled to see Liza. Her young ones were quite overcome by the importance of the occasion, especially Hazel.

All four youngsters could not take their eyes off Optimus, they were not at all sure he was real.

The old owl made his way over to Liza and warmly welcomed her home. They stood chatting for a while.

Touched by his kindness, Liza lowered her eyes; ashamed of the trouble she'd caused her father and everyone else.

Her bowed head brought a smile to the owl's face. He quickly put her at ease. "We are delighted that you've returned to us, and your young ones," he said, glancing at little Hazel

Overawed by his presence, Hazel tried to hide behind her grandfather, much to his, and everyone else's amusement.

Young Corsi, though a little nervous, took it all in his stride.

Solo and Almond stayed with Pecan's young ones. They were all happy playing.

Once the initial greetings were over, Optimus, called the meeting to order, and handed straight over to King Flylord, who had been helped onto the stone platform.

The old King stood on shaky legs, closing his eyes he took a deep breath, and looked out over the assembled gathering. Seeing the expectant faces staring up at him, his heart raced.

Prince Soar moved alongside him. "Father, are you alright?"

Flylord nodded and shuffled to edge of the platform. Raising his voice, he said. "I would like to thank Optimus for arranging this meeting." Glancing at the great owl, he bowed his head, before turning to face his expectant audience. "As you know, my daughter Liza, and her young ones, have returned home. This brings me great joy, and I would like to thank you all for welcoming her." Spotting Liza in the throng, he smiled at her.

"We all make mistakes in life." Lowering his head, he said softly, "I have made more than most, but we no longer dwell on that, for we have forgiven each other, and moved on with our lives. This is as true for my daughter Liza, as it is for me."

Spontaneous clapping and shouts of agreement echoed round the Clearing.

Raising a paw, Liza brushed a tear from her eye.

Supported by his tail, King Flylord stood tall, raised his fore-paws and called for silence. "I have something else I wish to say. I am old now and my time is short."

Loud cries of protest interrupted him.

"Please, let me finish." Flylord turned to Soar. "My son has proved himself a true leader. He is the one to take my place. I shall rest easy knowing he is in control."

This time everyone voiced their agreement.

King Flylord rested a paw on Soar's shoulder, and raised his voice. "You who are of my family…my clan; do you accept Prince Soar as your king?"

The unanimous reply was so loud…sleeping birds took to the air in fright.

"Does everyone agree with this?" Flylord asked again.

The throng surged forward, their voices raised in agreement.

Optimus stepped forward, a solemn expression on his face. "It is so recorded. Prince Soar, son of King Flylord, is now the King in Tamwood forest, and the leader of all rats."

Loud clapping and shouts of joy filled the Clearing.

King Flylord embraced his son, before slowly leaving the platform and returning to his clan. He was greeted with affection and tears.

In his early years, King Flylord had ruled with absolute authority. Nevertheless, he'd kept his clan together…they had survived. However, since the Rat Run, the King had changed…they all had. Now, Flylord was known for his kindness and wisdom. Both he and his son Prince Soar were loved by all.

Soar stepped to the front of the platform, and looked out at the rats gathered before him. His eyes misted as they rested on his father. His heart thudded in his chest. "Thank you my father. I am honoured to accept the Kingship. I will do my best to be a wise and compassionate leader."

Supported by his tail, he stood on his back legs and for a moment gazed in silence at the assembled throng. "We are entering a new season in our lives. There are many young ones among us, which is a great blessing, for they bring strength to every clan gathered here. There will also be many challenges, which we will have to face and overcome together." Taking a breath, he swung his paws wide, his eyes searching the faces staring up at him. "We are clever and resourceful creatures. There is nothing we cannot do if we stick together. Our strength lies in unity and trust."

The rats listening clapped and shouted. "Soar! Soar!" His words filled them with confidence and hope.

Soar smiled. "I will finish with some words from the book of wisdom. Remember them and always be kind to one another. If you show love, your life is not wasted."

He paused for a moment. When he spoke again his voice echoed around the Clearing…it seemed to those watching, that he grew in stature. Raising his voice, he loudly proclaimed.

"When all is said, and when all is done, there is only one thing that matters. Were my motives true, were my motives inspired by love? When all is said, and when all is done, love is what is left of my life, when my life is gone."

As the last words faded, a heavy silence hung over the assembled rats. No one spoke. There was nothing more to be said.

Leaving the platform, Soar joined his father.

Optimus made a point of congratulating him. Letting it be seen by all…the great owl honoured the new King.

Optimus had a few words with King Flylord, before taking to the air.

Seed followed him. It had been an amazing night, but now the old pigeon was tired and keen to get home. She flew behind Optimus. They were both silent, deep in their own thoughts.

No one would ever forget the past few months, so much had taken place, so much had changed. All because one brave rat had been willing to risk his life for the sake of all the others, and do the Rat Run.

Back in the Council Clearing, the rats were saying their farewells, and drifting away to their homes.

Liza smiled; she knew returning home was the right thing to do. "Thank you Chester," she said softly. "I hope you are well and happy." Gazing round the Clearing, she made eye contact with her father and bowed her head.

I have a lot to learn; she thought. *Nevertheless, this is where my lessons begin. I'm so glad for this opportunity to spend time with my father.*

Raising her head skyward, she murmured softly. "Thank you Soar, thank you Oracle, thank you Book of Wisdom."

The End

About the Author

Biography Y I Lee was born in Swindon Wiltshire, the eldest of three children. From a young age her greatest joy was to curl up with a good book. They became her escape from a troubled childhood. Over time she naturally progressed into writing. At the age of ten, she ambitiously attempted her first novel but quickly gave up. However, the seed was planted, and in the coming years in between a successful singing career she continued to put pen to paper, writing poetry and short stories. She's always had a great love for animals, especially horses. And thanks to a friend, she also grew to love Fancy rats, and spent a number of happy years breeding and showing them. Understandably, horses and rats often find their way into her books.

Y I Lee and her husband Keith live in the UK, in the beautiful county of Warwickshire.

More Books By Y I Lee

A Rat and A Ransom

The Shadowed Valley

Through a Glass

Through a Glass : Gathering Storm

Acknowledgements

First and foremost, I thank God, who is the inspiration and encouragement for every book I write. I couldn't do it without Him.

My grateful thanks and appreciation go to David and Ruth Rhodes. Your input and editing skills are invaluable.

I would also like to thank, Jo Harrison for her brilliant formatting. I wouldn't be able to publish without her.

And grateful thanks to Rebecca Fyfe for the awesome book cover.

Last but not least, I thank my husband, Keith, for his unwavering support and encouragement.

Made in the USA
Monee, IL
10 January 2022